CW00472194

Harems, Hexes, & Hairy Housewives

Menopause, Magick, & Mystery, Volume 8

JC BLAKE

Published by Redbegga Publishing, 2023.

This is a work of fiction. Similarities to real people, places, or events are entirely coincidental.

HAREMS, HEXES, & HAIRY HOUSEWIVES

First edition. April 1, 2023.

To my family.

Chapter One

December in the village was a difficult month for the coven. Although we were looking forward to Yule, there was the Night of Good Fires to endure.

"I do wish they would just stick to Bonfire Night and be done with it," complained Aunt Beatrice as she scooped another spoonful of apple and bramble crumble into Uncle Raif's bowl.

He poured a generous dollop of custard over the steaming pudding. "It's only one night," he placated.

"Indeed, but it is what it signifies, Raif," Aunt Beatrice continued. "I can't believe that after all this time the villagers celebrate the burning of witches with such relish!"

She sighed and sat down to the table then pushed her bowl of crumble away.

All eyes rested on her—pushing away crumble was a sign of deeply held concern of the most serious kind.

"Eat your crumble, Bea," Aunt Thomasin said with a quaver in her voice and a look of concern to my aunts.

"I feel it in my bones, sisters. Something terrible is coming our way." She rocked a little in her chair, sparks beginning to crackle above her head.

"Now, now, Bea," soothed Aunt Loveday with a concerned glance around the table. "There's really nothing to worry about."

"None at all," added Aunt Euphemia then scooped a spoonful of crumble into her mouth. "Mmm! Delicious. You've outdone yourself this time, Beatrice."

"Eat up, before your crumble goes cold," said Aunt Thomasin as though talking to a child.

Aunt Beatrice continued to ignore her crumble. A spark shot from her head, arcing as a flare before disappearing with a pop.

Uncle Raif rolled his eyes, scooped the final two spoons of crumble into his mouth in quick succession, thanked Aunt Beatrice for a wonderful meal, then exited the kitchen with the excuse of having some paintings to swot up on before finalising a price for the local antiques dealer. Since his near miss with death at the hands of Hegelina Fekkitt, Uncle Raif had launched himself into a number of new hobbies, or resurrected old interests, and was often away from home shooting, riding his motorbike along the winding roads of the undulating local hills, or visiting art galleries and museum exhibits. He specialised in the Renaissance. 'It reminds me of my youth,' he had said several nights before, 'but it's sad to see old friends hung on the walls of museums.' He'd given a soft chuckle. 'Mind you, some of them should have been hanged from a gibbet!'

With Uncle Raif gone, the mood in the kitchen grew serious.

"What is it, Beatrice?" Aunt Loveday questioned. "I have not seen you this concerned for more than a decade."

"Not since that incident with Filbert Osmond," added Aunt Thomasin.

Aunt Beatrice shivered. "It is exactly that! Oh, I have been having terrible dreams ..."

"Premonitions?"

Aunt Thomasin sighed. "Not again!"

"Well, sometimes they come true," said Aunt Beatrice in a defensive tone.

"But mostly not," retorted Aunt Thomasin.

"Well, this time, I feel it in my bones!" she protested.

"Ignore her, Beatrice," said Aunt Loveday. "Tell us about your dreams."

"Hetty Yikk-"

"Hsst!" The air crackled as my aunts expressed their dissatisfaction.

"Now, now, sisters, let us not overreact," schooled Aunt Loveday. "Beatrice is only relating a dream."

"She claims it is a premonition—a prophecy," Euphemia said with a flicker of fear.

"We will not know that until it happens," counselled Aunt Loveday. "Proceed, Beatrice."

"I sense her!" she said with a dramatic scan of the room. "As though she is lurking in the corners of this very room."

"Hsst!"

The lights flickered and the flames in the hearth grew low, hugging the logs.

"Sisters!" Aunt Loveday reprimanded. "Keep your heads. Now Beatrice," she said, returning her attention to the petite witch now quivering beneath a halo of sparking energy, "you know that is impossible. Hetty Yikk-"

"Hsst!"

Aunt Loveday threw Aunt Euphemia a disapproving frown then continued. "The black witch is dead."

"Isn't she the reason the villagers hold the Night of Good Fires?" I asked.

"Exactly! She was burned at the stake many years ago."

"1487," stated Aunt Thomasin. "I remember it well."

"As though it were yesterday," said Beatrice in a loud and stagey whisper.

"Well then, you very well remember that she is dead and can do no more harm to us."

"Was she your enemy?" I asked.

Aunt Loveday shook her head. "She grew to be a thorn in our side, but it was to the door of the village folk that she brought most trouble."

"She was a bad, bad woman," explained Aunt Thomasin.

"But a powerful witch!" Aunt Beatrice added.

"And a dead witch," Aunt Loveday said with a tone of finality. "Now, let us finish our crumble. I much prefer it warm." She ate another mouthful whilst giving a nod to us to follow suit. I ate mine whilst mulling over the story of Hetty Yikkar, a witch I knew little about, the topic being a taboo among my aunts.

To my knowledge, the Night of Good Fires was a centuries old ritual held at the end of November where the effigy of a witch was tied to a stake in the centre of the village and a fire lit beneath it. It was peculiar to Haligern village, the celebration of a particularly nasty crone who had tormented the village until they had captured her and burned her at the stake.

"How did they capture her?" I asked, speaking aloud. "If she was a witch who practiced dark magick."

All eyes fell upon me.

"And Yikkar ... does that mean she was related to-"

"She was a Pendlewick crone," said Aunt Loveday.

"What was a Pendlewick crone doing tormenting Haligern villagers?" I asked, now confused. "She was a long way from home."

"She's the reason the Pendlewick crones are a little testy towards us."

"Testy is an understatement although I do believe our score is settled, after we helped them with their problem."

"And Alice died on Haligern land too," I said, remembering the blackening body of Alice Yikkar I had discovered in the woodlands.

"Yes, but Hetty died in the village and not on Haligern land. She was burned to death by the villagers not us."

"But we helped the villagers defeat her," added Aunt Euphemia.

"Shh!" hissed Aunt Beatrice then scanned the corners of the room, the sparks beginning to crackle in her hair.

"Oh, Bea! There's no one else here."

Aunt Beatrice gave the corners of the room a furtive glance. "You never know who is listening."

"Pah!" said Aunt Thomasin. "Loveday has cleansed the cottage and refreshed the protective spell only this morning. There is your guarantee that nothing and no one is eaves dropping."

Aunt Beatrice relaxed and sat back in her chair then took another sip of tea. "I shall try to relax. Being so on edge is very wearing." She took another sip. "Ah! Such a good cup of tea. Everything seems better with tea," she said.

Murmured agreements among my aunts led to another round of pouring of tea and I suspected that a few extra drops of Aunt Thomasin's calming elixir had been added into the pot. As the tension in the room eased, and Aunt Beatrice's energy retreated, I ventured more questions about the witch burned at the stake only a few miles from the cottage.

"What was Hetty Yikkar doing in the village?" I asked, curious as to why a Pendlewick crone would have been here.

"Nefarious reasons," Aunt Euphemia answered.

Murmurs and nods of agreement passed among my aunts, and each took another sip of tea without explanation.

"Nefarious?" I nudged.

"Yes, nefarious," agreed Aunt Euphemia.

I sighed. "Nefarious how?"

"Dodgy."

"Yes, very dodgy."

"Oh, Thomasin, such a coarse way to describe it."

"More modern, I thought, given that Livitha does not seem to understand the meaning of the word 'nefarious.'"

"Of course I understand what the word means," I said taking offence. "I'm not stupid."

"No one has said that you are, dear."

"I was asking in what way she was being 'nefarious.'"

"Oh, in dodgy ways" Aunt Beatrice said then snorted into her tea.

My aunts glanced from one to the other then began to laugh.

I sighed and shook my head, wondering just how many extra drops of the calmative had been dropped into the pot.

"Forgive them, dear," said Aunt Loveday, "It's just their way of getting through the day."

Chapter Two

With the effigy of Guy Fawkes burned to a crisp beneath showers of iridescent fireworks on Bonfire Night behind us, and the horrors of watching Hetty Yikkar burn once again only a few weeks away, my aunts focused on producing lotions, potions, and salves for the apothecary whilst I busied myself serving our expanding base of customers. Many were repeat customers even beyond the village. Our 'Magical Menopause Rescue' hamper was a clear contender for most popular product with 'Elixirs of Youth' coming a close second.

Aunt Thomasin's success with her anti-ageing cream, even if it had been used as an excuse by Millicent to accuse the coven of dabbling in dark magick, had galvanised her into further improving her offering and she had converted the basement into a 'lab'.

On the morning after Aunt Beatrice's doom-laden worries about the influence of Hetty Yikkar from beyond the grave, footsteps ran up the stairs from the basement.

"I've done it!" Aunt Thomasin exclaimed as the cellar door banged against the staircase.

Aunt Beatrice turned to the open kitchen door in expectation, and seconds later Aunt Thomasin stood within its frame, eyes glittering. Her aura shone with a bright and metallic green light. I stood mesmerised by swirling and sparkling energy as it rolled across her shoulders.

"I've had a breakthrough!" she exclaimed and stepped into the kitchen. Her hair was in disarray, and a dark smear of soot crossed her forehead. Her pinafore was scorched.

"Breakthrough, dear?" questioned Aunt Beatrice as she turned from stirring the pot of stew bubbling on the stove, spoon in hand.

"Beatrice! My floor!" reprimanded Aunt Euphemia as drips of thick brown and nutritious stew dripped to the tiles. "I only mopped it this morning."

Aunt Beatrice muttered, "Sorry!" then returned the spoon to the stew pot.

"Well, you've quite stolen Thomasin's thunder, sisters," said Aunt Loveday with a touch of disapproval. "Tell us, Thomasin, what breakthrough have you had?"

"My anti-ageing cream. Look!" From deep within the pocket at the front of her pinny she pulled out a frog. Glassy-smooth and brilliant green, its skin glistened. For a moment it sat completely still, and I wondered if it were cut from gemstone. In the next moment it croaked then took a tentative step forward, ready to jump. Aunt Thomasin clamped her hand around it, slender fingers holding it in an embrace. "No, no, Pascal. You really mustn't jump."

Aunt Euphemia snorted.

Aunt Thomasin shot me a furtive glance and quickly looked away.

Aunt Beatrice tittered.

"I must say that Pascal is looking rather fine these days," Lucifer said as he slinked around my ankle. "Livitha, be a dear and pour me a saucer of port."

Was the frog my philandering ex-husband? "That is not Pascal! It cannot be."

Aunt Thomasin waved her free hand as though batting at a fly. "Of course it's not."

The frog looked strangely familiar.

"She's lying," Lucifer said in sly tones. "I'll tell you all about it if you pour me some-"

"If that's really Pascal-"

"Of course it's not Pascal," said Aunt Thomasin. "He was far uglier than this Pascal."

I took offence. "I know that you didn't like Pascal, but he wasn't unattractive."

"Until they turned him into a toad," snorted Lucifer.

"Oh, but my Pascal was ugly, very wrinkled and ugly only days ago," explained Aunt Thomasin.

Pascal croaked.

"I told you they were lying. If I were you-"

A wave of energy surged and Lucifer hissed, arched his back, and grew still, despite raised hackles. His mouth remained open, mid-comment.

"That's better," said Aunt Loveday as she flexed her hands and wriggled her fingers. "Now we can talk without constant interruptions."

"There will be hell to pay when he is released," warned Thomasin as Lucifer remained statue-like.

"He was getting above himself," replied Loveday. "You really must rein him in, Livitha. I won't tolerate a rude familiar. None of the others dare to speak that way."

Benny cawed in agreement from the windowsill then returned to looking outside whilst Bess sat to attention at Aunt Beatrice's feet, momentarily the best behaved familiar that any dog had ever been. Renweard, Aunt Loveday's wolfhound, looked up from his bed beside the fire then returned to sleep.

"He's not as bad as he was," I said in my defence.

"Have you been practicing levitation with him?" asked Aunt Loveday. "You were making great progress the last time I watched."

"I have, but it doesn't seem to faze him anymore."

"Then I suggest going heavy on transmogrification," she advised. "Turn him into a mouse for a day, something like that."

"I've tried it. He can turn himself back."

"Then I shall teach you a locking spell."

"And you accused Beatrice of stealing my thunder," said Aunt Thomasin holding up the emerald-green frog still clasped in her slender fingers.

Aunt Loveday opened her mouth as though to speak then let out a small laugh. "Yes, you are right, Thomasin. I'm sorry. Please, continue. Tell us about your cream."

Thomasin's annoyance was quickly forgotten as she continued to explain about her breakthrough. "Pascal," she said whilst stroking the top of the frog's head, "was a wrinkly toad, but after treatment with my newest potion, his skin has become beautifully smooth and youthful." She uncurled her fingers and held out the frog in the palm of her hand. His skin was glassily smooth.

"He does look beautiful," I agreed.

"Just think how wonderfully well this cream will sell at the shop."

I remembered Pascal, as he'd sat in a pool of his own clothes in the minutes after I'd turned him into a toad. The Pascal in Aunt Thomasin's hand looked eerily familiar, in a smooth and slimy way. "I don't think our customers want to be turned into frogs," I said.

Aunt Thomasin looked at me askance, momentarily confused.

"It's not going to turn anyone into a frog, dear," explained Aunt Loveday.

"Of course it's not! It's an anti-ageing cream. Pascal is still a toad; he just looks like a frog with all of his carbuncles smoothed out."

"I was distracted by thoughts of Pascal."

"It does bear a passing resemblance to him," said Aunt Euphemia.

"It's not actually Pascal, is it?" asked Aunt Beatrice as she held out her hand.

"Of course it's not," insisted Thomasin. "I have no idea where that disloyal and adulterous miscreant is."

"Probably at home," I said. *And probably with his newest girlfriend!*

The frog jumped into Aunt Beatrice's open palm as she threw me a pitying look. "How long will the effects last?" she asked holding the frog-toad up to eye level.

"Well!" exclaimed Aunt Thomasin. "That's the wonderful thing. His skin has been improving for the last two weeks with no sign of regression during that time."

"How do you know it's a male?" I asked, with lingering suspicion.

"I ... it's smaller than the other frogs. The females grow bigger."

"They look like brick outhouses compared to the males," said Aunt Beatrice with an air of authority.

"Anyway," said Aunt Thomasin, regaining her train of thought. "The cream has improved his skin each day. I stopped applying it for several days and there was no sign of regression."

"Wonderful!" exclaimed Loveday.

"Can I try it?" I asked. This morning I had become certain that the lines beneath my eyes were deepening.

Thomasin nodded. "You are youthful enough to get away with it. I fear if we used it then tongues would wag."

"And so close to the Night of Good Fires, we don't want to cause any suspicion in the village," said Aunt Loveday.

Her comment was met with a murmur of agreement and then low grumblings of doom.

"I hate it!" Aunt Euphemia blurted.

"Why, Euphemia, how can you be so scathing about my cream?"

"Not the cream. The villagers. The way they delight in burning the witch. I hate the Night of Good Fires. There's something glutinously horrid about the way they parade Hetty through the streets and then tie her to the stake. I won't be attending."

"Me neither," agreed Aunt Beatrice.

"I always have this sense of foreboding and dread at this time," added Aunt Thomasin.

"But nothing has ever happened," I said trying to soothe their concerns. "I've never known there to be a problem on that night."

"That's because we make sure we keep ourselves to ourselves in the month beforehand."

"Well ..." I thought back to the past months. Keeping a low profile was the last thing that the coven had done. "I'm sure this year will be no different."

"I'm not so sure," said Aunt Euphemia. "I overhead two gossips at the butchers when I collected our order last week." She pursed her lips.

"Well? What did you overhear, sister?"

"They were talking about Hrok."

Aunt Loveday let out a small groan. "I knew he would cause a stir. Those silly old crones." She tutted and shook her head.

"There's no fool like an old fool," agreed Aunt Beatrice.

"If they had only kept to a sensible age ..."

"They do look stunning," I said, remembering how the Slawston crones had been transformed from wrinkled old hags to long-limbed and nubile beauties. "Perhaps Hrok would be interested in your new cream. It would save some of his energy. He confided in me that transforming them was draining."

"It would have to be industrial strength!" Euphemia tittered.

"We'd have to scale up production," cackled Aunt Beatrice.

"What were the gossips saying?" I asked, curious to hear local opinion of Hrok and his harem of beautiful witches. More to the point—was his secret out?

"They are scandalised by their household arrangements. Apparently, they now refer to the house as the 'Playboy Mansion' and the Slawston sisters as 'Heffner's Harem'.

"Do they know that they *are* the Slawston sisters?"

Aunt Euphemia shook her head. "They made no mention of it, but then I've only heard a couple of gossips. There are many more in the village."

"Then I think we should have a special evening at the apothecary to take their mind off things."

"But you said we should lie low, Loveday."

"How modern you sound, Beatrice," said Loveday. "What I meant is that we should not raise our heads above the parapet. You more than anyone should know what happens if you do."

Aunt Beatrice rubbed her head as though remembering an old injury. "You're right but lying low is the same thing."

"I agree," said Aunt Euphemia.

"Is your cream ready for the ladies of the village, Thomasin?" asked Aunt Loveday ignoring their comments.

"It is," she beamed. "And we shall have Livitha as our poster girl."

The frog gave a loud 'grivit' and jumped from Aunt Beatrice's hand and onto Lucifer's back. Still under Aunt Loveday's spell, the feline could only shiver as the frog made its way through his fur to sit on his head. Just as the frog settled down, Lucifer made a low and rumbling yowl, and the latch of the front door lifted.

Chapter Three

The distinctive rustle of Mrs. Driscoll's raincoat being placed on a hook in the hallway was followed by the clop of her heels as she made her way to the kitchen. The room was suddenly a flurry of activity. Aunt Thomasin picked Pascal from Lucifer's head and placed him deep in her pinny pocket then began to sweep the floor. Aunt Loveday cleared the plates from the table. Aunt Euphemia took the dustpan and brush from beneath the sink and turned her attention to sweeping the hearth and adding several more logs to the fire. Aunt Beatrice filled the sink with hot water as I took the duster from the pantry and reached above the door to sweep away imaginary cobwebs.

"Good morning, ladies," Mrs. Driscoll said as she entered the kitchen. "My, you're all so busy this morning. You'll be putting me to shame!"

A chorus of 'Good morning!' followed and Mrs. Driscoll made her way to the cupboard under the sink and retrieved a tub of beeswax and a cloth. "Seeing as we did such a thorough job of cleaning last time, I thought I'd make a start on polishing the furniture."

"What a good idea, Mrs. Driscoll," Aunt Beatrice said. "I shall join you once I've washed up these breakfast pots."

"Hmm," Mrs. Driscoll said, hovering with the pot in her hand.

All eyes turned to her. She had something to say. Some gossip to impart.

"Would you like a cup of tea?" Aunt Beatrice asked, picking up on the signal.

"Oh, yes, please. I am parched."

"And biscuits?"

She glanced at her watch. "Well, it's not elevenses," she said, "but ... well, just one." Her smile broadened and she placed the pot of beeswax on the table along with the cloth and took a seat.

Aunt Beatrice filled the teapot with fresh leaves and boiling water and placed it at the centre of the table. "Oh, I have a treat for you today. I baked some of those biscuits you loved."

"Oh, did you? They were delicious."

After the last incident with Mrs. Driscoll, we had noticed a difference in her behaviour. Nothing extreme, just moments when she would zone out and stare across the room, dusting cloth in hand as though polishing the air, or with the vacuum cleaner held aloft. After some research, Aunt Loveday had diagnosed a case of 'slipped mind', an affliction that could befall a human who had come under the influence of magick. Poor Mrs. Driscoll had suffered on several occasions, at one point being possessed by the black witch Hegelina Fekkit. Hegelina had been punished though and now lived as a cursed goat along with Old Mawde and provided us with fresh milk daily. The biscuits were part of Mrs. Driscoll's therapy, made to a recipe Aunt Loveday had concocted after several hours of research poring through Alfred, her ancient grimoire.

"Thank you." Mrs. Driscoll took the offered biscuit from the plate. "Aren't you having one?"

"Oh, there was only one left," Aunt Beatrice lied. "We ate the rest." Aunt Beatrice joined her at the table whilst we continued the charade of looking busy.

"Well," Mrs. Driscoll said after a second sip of tea. "There's much ado in the village."

"There is?" asked Aunt Thomasin looking up from her sweeping with a little too much enthusiasm.

"Yes!" replied Mrs. Driscoll. "There's newcomers in the village."

"Oh?"

I swept at a cobweb in the corner of the room whilst zoning in on the conversation.

"And they're causing such trouble as you would not believe."

I imagined a family with young and unruly teenagers, riding bikes or scooters, and weaving among the pensioners along the village paths. "Is it a family?"

Mrs. Driscoll shook her head. "You couldn't call them that, no. Although they might call themselves *the* family." She raised her brows. "The word is that they're part of a cult!"

"A cult!" I exclaimed. "In Haligern?"

Mrs. Driscoll nodded. "Yes! It's hard to believe, I know, we live in such an ordinary village."

I couldn't agree that the village was ordinary but didn't challenge her.

"They call themselves the 'Purity Revivalists'. Which is strange, if you ask me."

It was agreed that the name was strange.

"And what do they do, these 'Purity Revivalist'?"

"Revive purity," snorted Aunt Beatrice.

"They have a motto, apparently," continued Mrs. Driscoll.

"Which is?"

"'Purity Cleanses & Brings Joy.'

"How very odd."

Mrs. Driscoll nodded. "What's more surprising, given the degeneracy of our age, is that they do seem to be popular among the housewives. They hold weekly meetings at the village hall. And services of an evening."

I began to wonder what contact Mrs. Driscoll had had with the cult. "Have you been to any meetings?"

"Oh, no. not me, but my Agnes went to one of their services the other night."

"She did not!" exclaimed Aunt Euphemia.

"She did, Euphemia," replied Mrs. Driscoll. "She did."

Concerned glances passed among my aunts. Agnes had an unfortunate history of exploring new ideas.

"Is that wise?" asked Aunt Loveday.

An interest in witchcraft had led Agnes to steal Arthur, Aunt Loveday's powerful and priceless grimoire, as well as a cild ælfen, the larval stage of a fairy's child. The memories brought with them a frisson of fear as I remembered the dark entities that had almost broken through the protective membrane that separated our world from theirs when the grimoire had been misused. "I hope Agnes isn't going to get too involved."

"Don't worry, ladies. My Agnes only went along to be nosey."

Aunt Thomasin sighed. "Well, that is a relief to know."

Aunt Loveday remained guarded. "Perhaps you should have a chat with her, Livitha," she suggested. "You helped her ... before."

"Oh, there's no need to worry," insisted Mrs. Driscoll. "She really is just being nosey and bringing back all the gossip to me. I wouldn't know anything about what they're up to otherwise."

"How is Agnes?" Loveday asked.

"Oh, she's fine. Completely recovered after her ordeal. And not about to be tricked into any cult, I can assure you. Particularly not one that insists you take daily showers. She's a clean girl, don't get me wrong, but daily showers in cold water!" Mrs. Driscoll shuddered. "No thank you!"

"Is that part of their teaching? To take cold showers."

"Yes. The other thing they insist upon is celibacy, unless married of course. Agnes is a good girl, so I'm sure that wouldn't be an issue, but ... cold showers! Ugh!" She shuddered for dramatic effect.

"Hmm," murmured Aunt Loveday.

"And you're to say certain phrases before you do anything," she added.

"A classic sign of a cult," said Aunt Beatrice with authority.

"Such as?" pressed Aunt Loveday.

"Oh, let me see ... Yes! You must say, 'Water cleanse my skin and my mind, and make me pure,' before you step into the shower. And then you're to turn around thrice and recite 'purity cleanses' whilst you're beneath the freezing water. And you have to stay under for at least thirty seconds."

"Peculiar."

"Sounds dangerous! You could slip circling in the shower," declared Aunt Beatrice. "I much prefer baths."

This statement was followed by murmurs of agreement about the preference for bathing. Aunt Thomasin declared that the best form of bathing was beneath a waterfall. "I have never been as clean in my life as I have been after bathing beneath a waterfall," she declared to a look of astonishment from Mrs. Driscoll.

"Without clothes?" she asked.

"Oh, yes," replied Thomasin. "Completely in the nude."

Mrs. Driscoll's brows raised a fraction.

"Oh, it's wonderfully freeing to be naked on a moonlit night," Aunt Thomasin said, losing herself to memories, a smile broadening across her face. "I remember Percival Longbeard and-"

"So, this cult, Mrs. Driscoll," Aunt Loveday said in a voice loud enough to drown out Aunt Thomasin's account of a passionate encounter with a well-endowed and muscular paramour of her youth, "who is in charge?"

Mesmerised by Aunt Thomasin's reminiscences, it took Mrs. Driscoll several moments before Loveday's words entered her awareness. "Oh! The cult. Yes, well, she's new to the village. An older woman, but very pretty. I don't know much about her, other than that, I'm afraid. But there is another thing," she said. "I'm not sure if you've heard, but we seem to have a playboy mansion in the village."

"Oh?" said Aunt Loveday feigning ignorance.

"Yes! It's quite the scandal. It was even before Prudence arrived, but now that she's preaching about purity and being celibate unless married, well, the issue has become quite heated."

This corroborated the gossip Aunt Euphemia had overheard. My concern was that Hrok's secret, that he was a powerful sorcerer using magick to turn the Slawston crones' biological clocks back hundreds of years and transform them into beautiful young women, would be discovered. The discovery, particularly so close to the Night of Good Fires, could be incendiary. I decided to pay him a visit and warn him of the rising tensions as soon as I had time.

Chapter Four

After Mrs. Driscoll had finished polishing and left the cottage, we turned our attention back to Aunt Thomasin's miraculous anti-ageing cream.

"If it works, it could make us famous!" Aunt Euphemia said in an excited tone.

Aunt Beatrice shuddered. "That is the last thing that we want, sister. Particularly so close to the Night!"

"Our name is spreading," I added. "Our customer base reaches from one end of the island to the other. We even had an order from Texas yesterday."

"Texas! Isn't that abroad? In the New World?"

"Oh, Beatrice, you know that it is!"

"Well, it's part of the Empire then. Do we class that as abroad?"

I shook my head. For all of my aunts' knowledge, their reclusive lives sometimes curtailed it in peculiar ways.

"Not anymore. They overthrew the British in the eighteenth century," I said. "Texas is part of the United States of America now."

"Oh," she said. "Well, I stopped reading the newspapers a long time ago. It's hard to keep up with it all."

"Ignore her," said Aunt Thomasin, "I really don't believe that she doesn't know that."

"Well, anyway, there's far too much going on in our own lives to worry about countries thousands of miles away," Aunt Beatrice retaliated. "And we do have other realms to worry about."

"There you have it!" stated Aunt Euphemia. "She is feigning ignorance to segway the Academy into the conversation!"

"Beatrice, if you're going to start going on about the Academy again, I shall ... Well, can we please have one morning without you talking about Grimlock Yikkar and your work at the Academy? Please?"

Aunt Beatrice sniffed. "I only talk about it because I find it all so fascinating."

"Yikkar," I said. "Grimlock Yikkar must have been a relation of Hetty's then."

"Her brother," explained Aunt Thomasin. "They were very close at one point, but when she began dabbling in dark magick he had to turn his back on her."

"Hsst! Don't mention that name. Not at this time of the year."

"Oh, Beatrice," sighed Aunt Thomasin. "You have become such a worry wart since you started working."

"I've just learned a lot."

"Well, whatever you have learned has made you paranoid. Let us focus on the task in hand, which is to make a batch of my new and improved cream. We have an open evening to prepare for."

"So close to the Night?" asked Aunt Beatrice.

"Yes, if we are to help Hrok and the Slawston crones."

"It is short notice," I said. "Perhaps we should wait a while. How about in a few weeks, ready for Yule?"

"I thought that we had agreed to hold an event to help take the villager's attention away from Hrok," said Aunt Thomasin.

It was agreed that the promotion should go ahead in the interest of helping Hrok, and the kitchen became a hive of activity as the production process to create the miraculous anti-ageing cream began. I was given a list of magically infused herbs to collect from the storerooms whilst the fire was stoked, and the pot-bellied cauldron brought in from the shed and hung from a large hook within the chimney.

Water began to bubble, and Aunt Thomasin threw in the first herbs, murmuring an incantation of ancient words, her grimoire laid open on her knees as she sat beside the fire. Steam, laced with ribbons of iridescence, rose from the pot.

Whilst she worked, I was her apprentice and passed her the herbs as directed. She instructed me to write down the charms she was reciting along with instructions for their addition to the pot. "The grimoires are full of charms and spells, Livitha," she said, "but much of what I know is in my memories. Take note and scribe them to your grimoire tonight."

As I passed her the herbs and noted down the charms, my mind turned to Garrett. Each time he came to mind, I felt a thrill of excitement. We were to be married. It seemed like a miracle that at the age of fifty I was going to be married to the man I loved most in the world. A man I had loved since we first met as teenagers and when we were both oblivious to our magical inheritance.

Garrett's proposal had been one of the most joyous moments of my life but was quickly followed by doubt. Not that I doubted I wanted to marry Garrett. I did, but there were potential obstacles in our way. Or rather, one potential obstacle—Garrett's mother. According to protocol, she had to give permission for us to marry and Uncle Tobias was to petition her on our behalf. That permission was required, and that it was not just some archaic formality, had come as a shock. Pascal and I had married without even thinking of asking for permission but for marriage among our own kind, those with magical abilities whose lineage went back thousands of years, the rules were different. A marriage between the clans, particularly one as important as the Blackwoods held themselves to be, was a serious business.

Aunt Thomasin picked up on the change in my mood immediately.

"Is something on your mind, Livitha?" she asked as I sat pen in hand whilst gazing into the fire.

"No," I replied without thought.

"Well, that's a bald-faced lie," she chuckled. "Now, tell me, what ails you?"

"Nothing is ailing me."

"You're not ill, then."

"No."

"Then what is it? You're sitting there gazing into the fire with a look of forlorn distress upon your pretty face. I have grown concerned."

I snapped out of my reverie. "I didn't mean to worry you, it's just ..." I sighed. "Garrett's mother!"

Aunt Thomasin's brow creased. "Has she replied to Tobias' petition?"

"Not with an answer," I replied. "But she's spending Yule at Blackwood Manor. Uncle Tobias is to petition her formally then."

"Ah, and you're worried that she won't accept you. Pass me eight sprigs of horsetail, dear."

I counted out the sprigs of dried horsetail and passed them across. She threw them into the pot, and I noted down the charm as she recited.

"I suppose I am worried," I replied as iridescent steam swirled above the cauldron. "It seems so old-fashioned and being fifty years old a bit ... silly."

"You are a child, Livitha. Fifty is nothing for us. Care must be taken on choosing a bride or a groom. Our marriages last for centuries and can bring great fortune to the families or great calamity. The Blackwoods have already borne great damage from poor choices."

"Great!" I said, the sense of doom a little more dense.

"Now, now, don't be like that. There is no reason why she would give a formal objection to the match." She stirred the pot. "I can understand your concern, child, but you must not dwell upon it. In truth, these things are often just a formality, his mother always was a stickler for protocol. I cannot think that she will be anything but thrilled at the news Garrett has proposed. You are Livitha Erikson, daughter of Soren. They will consider it a privilege. And anyhow, what's not to like," she said with a gesture towards me.

I could think of a hundred self-pitying reasons why Garrett's mother would not accept me but remained silent.

"She will come to love you as we do, dear. That is our way. Once a person, man, woman, or child, is taken into our family they become as one with us ... which is why so much care must be taken when choosing a bride or a groom. We have put aside our prejudices against the Blackwoods ... they, I am sure, will put their prejudices against us aside too."

"The Blackwoods are prejudiced against the Eriksons?"

Aunt Thomasin nodded. "They may well be, but the Blackwoods are cursed, and we are not, so I really cannot think that there will be an issue towards accepting you into their family."

She gave the steaming brew of herbs and magic another stir, then declared that it must be left to bubble whilst I was left pondering all the reasons Garrett's mother could object to me.

"Hsst!" declared Aunt Beatrice as she stepped back into the kitchen with a disapproving frown. "Listen to that nonsense!

Chapter Five

The following morning, with the pots of cream cooled, their lids tightened, and labels attached, they were boxed and placed on the kitchen table ready to be taken to the shop. As nominated guinea pig/poster girl, I had smeared a generous dollop onto my face, allowing Aunt Thomasin to rub it into my skin, to make sure that it soaked into 'all the nooks and crannies'. Aunt Thomasin had forced me to examine my face in a hand mirror whilst standing at the kitchen window where the light was 'honest' so that I could see just how 'ravaged by time' my face had become over the years. Apparently, this would enable me to compare it to the new and improved version that her miracle potion would produce.

The light at the window had been more than honest, it was harsh, and I had flinched at the rosy-cheeked reflection staring back at me. There were several red patches on my cheeks and a spidery cluster of capillaries, along with unsightly open pores at the sides of my nose. The bags beneath my eyes were indeed baggy and the crows' feet at the side of my eyes had grown deeper since I'd last taken a close inspection. The light had also revealed a number of straggly hairs beneath my chin and a wispy moustache of light-coloured hairs along my top lip. I withheld a disappointed groan and glanced at my aunts. How did they manage to look so youthful? Yes, they looked to be in their seventies, an age magically induced to help them fit in, but their skin was beautiful, unblemished, and without sag, with no evidence of stray hairs at all. At the rate I was ageing, I would morph into a haggard crone within a decade or two. Their secret was magick that I had to learn—and fast!

There was one upside to growing old and coming into my powers. My hair now had a fabulous streak of white that reminded me of Frankenstein's bride. Unfortunately, the sight of my ageing face in the mirror and its reflected and cruel HD-ready light also induced the same horror-struck look as the bride when she'd first been introduced to her groom.

"Don't worry dear," said Aunt Euphemia picking up on my energy. "The cream will fix it."

"And once you've become a crone then the whiskers will disappear," said Aunt Beatrice. "And yes, I did hear your thoughts, but given just how loud you are, I can be forgiven. It's not snooping if someone is yelling in your ear!"

Despite the unflattering reflection, applying the cream was a pleasurable experience and, as my skin warmed beneath Aunt Thomasin's fingers, I felt hopeful. Her own skin looked dewy and clear of blemishes. How long would it take before I became a crone?

"Thomasin was a great beauty," said Aunt Beatrice. "But you'll look beautiful too. And you've only just come into your powers, dear. It takes an age to become a crone."

I resolved to discover a way to shut my aunt out from my thoughts and checked again in the mirror. The difference was clear. The redness in my cheeks had reduced and the bagginess beneath my eyes had smoothed. It was still there, but less noticeable. Even the hairs on my top lip seemed less obvious and the open pores had shrunk. "I can't believe it has worked so quickly!" I enthused. "It's quite amazing."

Aunt Thomasin beamed. "I added a little extra yarrow for tightening."

"They use yarrow to tighten vaginas, you know."

Aunt Euphemia, mid-sip, snorted and tea sprayed from her nostrils.

"We should offer the cream at the apothecary—as a tightener. I'm sure it would sell," Aunt Beatrice added.

I felt a flush rise to my cheeks. "I ... I'm sure it would."

"Nothing worse than a saggy-"

"Beatrice, did you say that Grimlock was visiting?"

She frowned and shook her head. "No. I don't believe I did, although it's possible that he will. You know what he's like. He just pops up out of nowhere."

"Literally," I said remembering the last time the ancient Vardlokkur had magically appeared in the kitchen from the chimney, complete with deer antler headdress, and blown soot and ash across the room. I took a final look at my new and improved face then placed the mirror on the table.

"You are positively glowing, Livitha," said Aunt Thomasin.

"It is working," agreed Aunt Euphemia, "I can see the difference already."

Aunt Thomasin tapped the cardboard box on the table. "Are you going to take these along to the shop? When shall we run our promotion? I think making quite a fuss of it – if making a splash to avert the villagers' thoughts from Hrok and his harem is the objective – would be the thing to do."

"How about Thursday evening?" I suggested.

"Thor's day. Yes, I agree," said Aunt Euphemia. "A perfect day for making a storm," she said then cackled at her joke.

"Thor's Day it is then," agreed Aunt Thomasin.

With the date for the promotion being set, I made my way to the apothecary.

I arrived just before ten o'clock, which was when the shop opened, and was relieved to find no one waiting outside. Often, I would be a few minutes late to a queue of customers giving me no time to organise myself or ease into the day. Ideally, I liked to set the log burner to work and be sat having a cup of tea in a warmed shop before the first customer arrived. This morning, I was able to achieve that happy state of mercantile bliss.

With the logs aflame in the burner and the kettle ready to boil, I set about dusting and restocking the shelves before checking for any orders that had come in online. There were several and as I began to assemble the first order, another hamper full of menopausal goodies, Aunt Loveday surprised me by walking through the door. It was unusual for her to be at the shop, preferring to work behind the scenes at the cottage and tending to the herbs or delving within the hidden pages of Arthur for new charms to add magic to our potions.

"Are you busy?" she asked as I placed another jar in the box and ticked it off my list.

"Just another menopause hamper."

"Are they still selling well?" she asked.

"Very well," I replied.

"I won't keep you. "I've only popped in. I had a client this morning – a land blessing – and thought I'd see how it's all running." She scanned the shop. "It does look welcoming.

You're doing a wonderful job of creating inviting and positive energy."

"Thanks," I replied then offered her a cup of tea.

With the tea made, we chatted about the promotional evening and which products were selling well and which could be improved.

"I know it's controversial," she said, "but I think Beatrice's idea about the tightening cream is a good one."

"I do too," I replied, "although I'm not sure how to promote it. I'd rather not have an open evening … or posters in the window declaring the launch of a cream to tighten women's nether regions. I'm sure the locals would find that embarrassing."

"Hmm. A simple display with a note beside explaining the benefits should be sufficient. No need to shout about it through a loud hailer," she smiled.

"When it's ready, I can send out an email to announce it to our customers—something subtle," I suggested.

"That sounds like a good idea," she agreed and took another sip of tea.

As I collected a jar of moisturiser for ageing skin from the shelf to put into the hamper, I noticed Hrok outside. Aunt Loveday followed my gaze.

"Is that Hrok talking to a woman?" she asked.

"I think so."

"He seems very familiar with her."

"Do you think he's chatting her up?"

"Courting her do you mean?"

"Erm, not quite, but flirting … he does look as though he's flirting with her."

Aunt Loveday continued to watch. "I think you are right, Livitha. He does seem to be overly familiar with the woman. And ... is he going to kiss her?"

Hrok leant towards the woman, but rather than kissing her, the woman pulled back her sleeve to reveal a watch.

"Ah! He's just asking her the time."

I recognised the woman as one of our customers. "That's Mandy Braithwaite. I used to go to school with her. She's a pharmacist and married to the manager of the pub," I said. "She often comes into the shop."

"So, she has a husband."

"Yes, and I've never heard her say a negative word about him."

"Happily married then."

As I agreed that she could be happily married, Mandy pulled down her sleeve, Hrok nodded, and they parted company. He waved as she walked away. My thoughts turned to Garrett.

Would he become a lothario like Hrok? A stone seemed to sink in my stomach. Would he live as long as me? Dread fell over me like a wet and smelly cloth; what if he wasn't gifted with longevity? Panic set in. What if he aged like Uncle Raif and I had to wait for him to pass and then be left alone for aeons?

I glanced at Aunt Loveday. Her marriage to Uncle Raif was centuries old, but the attack she suffered at the hands of Hegelina Fekkit made clear just how vulnerable he was, how quickly he would age and die, once her magic began to fail which, at some point, it surely would. Was that Garrett's fate too? Or was there enough of his mother's heritage within him.

"Why, Livitha!" Loveday exclaimed as our eyes met. "Whatever is the matter? The very air is crackling, and your aura has grown quite black."

"Uncle Tobias," I blurted. "How old is he?"

A bemused frown fell upon Loveday's face.

"Well ... He's of a similar age to Euphemia, if memory serves."

"So, hundreds of years!"

Loveday glanced about the shop. "Don't tell her I said so, but yes."

Relief washed away the damp and smelly blanket. "Thank Thor and Odin and Freya, and-"

Loveday's brow cleared and sadness flickered in her eyes. "Ah, you were wondering if Garrett would ... if he was like us."

I nodded. "Yes!"

She smiled. "Fear not, dear child. Garrett is a Blackwood. His great, great grandfather came to this island with me. We are the same. Them and us. He is not like my darling Raif."

Her attention was drawn back to the scene outside, where Hrok was speaking to another woman, this time one with a child in a pushchair. Once again, he appeared to be asking for the time.

"He really is the most outrageous flirt. So many of our men are. It comes from living such a long time and excessive virility."

"Oh," I said desperately thinking of how to change the subject; discussing men's virility with my aunt was not something I wanted to do. I was still overcoming the shock of listening to Aunt Thomasin talk about her 'well-endowed, if you know what I mean' lover and Aunt Beatrice claiming that yarrow was an excellent herb for tightening the vagina.

"They get hooked on the variety, I suppose," Aunt Loveday continued. "In my experience-"

"I've been thinking about yarrow," I blurted. *Damn! Bad choice.*

"Oh?"

"It's tightening properties ... I think they would be an excellent addition to the menopausal package we offer. It is our most popular product."

"Yes. Hmm. I think that would be a good addition. Have you also considered something for dryness in that region. Could that be added?"

"Is that a thing?" I asked with a grimace.

Aunt Loveday chuckled. "Ah, Livitha, you have so much to learn. After being in this business for as long as I have, nothing shocks me anymore, and yes, dryness for ladies during the menopause can be a terrible affliction. I have a wonderful recipe for making an excellent lotion. But ... I think that the time has come for you to spread your wings in that area."

"You want me to create a cream for dryness ... down there?"

She nodded. "Yes. And your first port of call should be the leaf of the red raspberry. It is the quintessential women's herb."

I made a note on the pad beside the till.

"It alleviates terrible female ailments such as menstrual cramps and vaginal dryness. It also helps to strengthen the womb and increase fertility."

I jotted the ailments and beneficial properties down.

"But of course, you will need to discover when the best time for picking is and which charms to call upon to infuse your lotion with."

"How will I know if it works?"

"You shall have to try it out."

I now wanted the floor to swallow me. "But I don't ... have vaginal dryness!"

As I uttered those words, the bell tinkled above the door, and Garrett stood in the doorway.

His gaze caught mine and I realised the moment our eyes locked that he had overheard.

"Ah ... oh ... I can come back another time," he said, a flush already on his cheeks.

For the love of Thor, may thunder strike the ground and the floor open, and swallow me down. Right now!

Chapter Six

Aunt Loveday left the shop, leaving me to explain to Garrett about the suggestion we create creams for 'women's issues'. He replied with an 'Ah!', grimaced, and changed the subject.

"I thought we could go for lunch at the café. I was in the area ..."

"I'd love to," I replied then launched into a monologue about what tasty meals they served and how much I enjoyed the coffee the last time we'd visited. Before he had a chance to answer, I launched into talking about the weather, hoping that a rapid fire of questions would lead him away from thoughts of dry and tight lady parts.

"It's already noon," he said with a look of befuddled amusement as I began to talk about how much an early frost improved Brussel sprouts. "Shall we go for lunch now?"

"Sure," I replied. "I'll grab my coat."

I made my way from the counter to the back room to retrieve my coat and scarf. When I returned, Garrett's attention was fixed to a scene on the pavement across the road.

"Does he just hang around the village all day waiting for women?" he asked.

"Who?" I asked pushing an arm through a coat sleeve as I reached his side.

Hrok stood on the other side of the road talking to another woman, one I recognised as a customer who had been into the shop last week for anti-ageing cream. I'd been struck by the smoothness of her skin. She was a little younger than me but with no sign of wrinkles or unwanted facial hair. As Hrok spoke, she pulled up her sleeve and glanced at her watch.

"I saw him talking to women earlier." He turned to me with a frown. "Why is he standing opposite the shop? Do you think he's trying to get your attention?"

The idea hadn't crossed my mind. "No! Why on earth would he?"

"Well, you're an attractive woman, Liv," he said, catching my gaze.

He held my eyes for a moment before returning his attention to Hrok.

Was he accusing me of something? "I don't know what he's up to," I replied. "But it really has absolutely nothing to do with me. We were watching him earlier. He seems to be asking the women the time."

"Is he ... alright?"

"Alright?"

"Yes. It's odd behaviour. I'm wondering if the strain of running his harem is getting to him. The amount of energy he uses must be off the charts."

I nodded, remembering the complaints of exhaustion he'd made. "I think it's wearing him down."

"No fool like an old fool," Garrett said. "You couldn't pay me to have more than one woman to deal with."

"I'll take that as a compliment," I laughed.

He turned to me with surprise. "Oh, well I just meant that it must be a burden—having six women to ... deal with. And, of course, you're the only woman I'd ever want."

He slipped a reassuring arm across my shoulder. I leant into him, and we stood in a moment of mutual affection whilst watching Hrok speak to the next woman who approached him.

"I think I know why he's standing there. Women are coming out of the café and further along the road is the village hall. They hold Pilates and flower arranging classes there on some mornings."

"So, a steady stream of attractive women," Garrett said. "Is he recruiting, do you think?" he asked with a dry tone.

I snorted with laughter.

"Well, it's either that or he has become obsessed by the time." Garrett reached for the door handle but as he was about to pull it open, a man emerged from the café and strode up to Hrok and the woman.

"Oh, dear," I said. "It looks like Hrok has a rival!"

The man, broad-shouldered and in workman's cargo-style trousers complete with tool belt and plaid shirt, stood beside the woman. He slipped a possessive arm across her shoulder. The man leant forward in an aggressive stance and Hrok raised his hands as though in surrender and took a step back. The man took a step forward and Hrok took a step onto the road. The man shook a fist then began to walk away, his arm now slipped through the crook of the woman's.

"That told him then. He'll get a rep-"

Garrett stalled as the man, who had gained speed, slammed directly into a lamppost. As the man staggered back, his head bouncing from the wooden post, Hrok smirked.

Behind me fairies chittered, hovering at my shoulder to watch the comical scene outside. A brush of air against my cheek was followed by the buzzing of wings as a dozen tiny creatures swooped above us.

With his shoulders heaving with laughter, Hrok watched as the man turned in dazed confusion, unsure of which direction to walk. The sorcerer's smug satisfaction quickly turned to shock as the woman jolted forward as though pushed and fell into the road. In the next moment, her skirt lifted up, revealing her knickers, and landed on her thigh as though flicked up.

Squeals of mirth erupted above us, and the fairies swooped in an excited murmuration.

The man staggered, walking away from the woman before knocking into a wall, whilst she crawled back onto the pavement on all fours.

"Did Hrok do that?" Garrett asked with a doubtful tone.

"I don't think he did," I said as Hrok offered his hand to the woman as she began to stagger to her feet. "It looked as though she tripped."

"Or was pushed."

A fairy flew to the window, its tiny hands resting on the glass. It shivered before chittering. The other fairies followed. Rising up, then down, they hovered like hummingbirds drinking nectar from an open flower as they peered through the glass.

From the corner of my eye I noticed a figure but it disappeared and I was left with the impression that it could have been a woman. The fairies erupted in a frenzy of noise then rose as one to the ceiling before darting across the room and back to the grandfather clock.

"Something has spooked them," Garrett quipped as he watched the fairies' progress across the room to the grandfather clock then returned his attention to Hrok and the couple. The woman pulled her arm from Hrok's grip, then made her way to the man now leaning up against the wall.

"Hrok should be careful how he uses his magick," Garrett said as he pulled the shop door open. "He'll make enemies around here otherwise."

From the café window, several women watched the commotion, lips pursed, their eyes hard.

"I think he already has," I said.

Before we had a chance to cross, Hrok walked a little further up the road then crossed it before disappearing around a corner.

As we entered, the café was filled with chattering voices, and a single table remained empty. Thankfully, it was the one furthest away from the other diners. As we sat down, I checked my watch.

"Busy?"

I nodded. "Yes, I've got orders to pack up before the post-office closes and Loveday has set me on a quest. I've got research to do."

"The ..." He nodded downwards with a barely suppressed smile. "Cream?"

I pressed my lips together. "Yes, but I'd rather not talk about it, if you don't mind."

"I'd rather you didn't too, so we can agree on that."

"We can." I took the menu from the holder on the table and began to scan the dishes offered.

"So ... would the cream tighten the whole area?"

I cast him a glance from beneath my lashes, hysteria beginning to bubble. "I really couldn't say."

"So ... you haven't tested it then."

I shot him a glare then batted the menu at him. He burst into laughter. "Just my way of getting through the day," he chuckled. "Although I bet if you put it on pre-order it would sell like hotcakes. I bet every woman in this room would buy a jar—or two."

"Stop it!" I whispered, suppressing a snort. "Let's order." I passed him the menu.

A waitress approached our table, notebook and pen in hand, but before she asked us what we'd like to order, she narrowed her eyes and said, "You that lady from the witches' shop?"

Garrett caught my eyes, a crease appearing between his brows. I threw him a quick, placating, smile. "I manage Haligern Apothecary," I replied in a friendly tone.

Her lips pursed momentarily. "What would you like? Today's special is carrot and coriander soup served with olive focaccia."

"Sounds good," Garrett said, "But I'd like a baked potato."

We both ordered a baked potato with a topping of baked beans and tuna and a side-serving of coleslaw, and the waitress turned away with a definite strop.

"What was that about?" he asked.

It was almost a rhetorical question; Garrett knew that our presence in the village wasn't embraced by all of its inhabitants.

"I don't know, I replied although memories of the mob that had gathered outside our door after a sink hole had swallowed a controversial new housing estate surfaced. "I can't think that we've done anything to upset them—at least not in the past few weeks. It's been months since last time."

"Hmm," Garrett murmured but remained silent as the waitress brought a steaming pot of tea and placed it along with cups, saucers, and a small jug of milk, on the table. We chatted for several minutes whilst we waited for the leaves to infuse. Garrett hated a weak cup of tea. A glint in his eye gave me a warning. I knew exactly what he was thinking. On several occasions he pressed his lips together and looked over my shoulder to the wall beyond. I shot him a good-humoured but warning glare. He would get weeks of amusement from overhearing the conversation about the nether-region cream. However, when his face grew serious, I knew that something was troubling him.

"What is it?"

He looked thoughtful then said, "I've got to go on a course next week."

"Another one?" I asked, surprised. "You've been on at least three in the last six months."

He nodded. "Yep, and I can't get out of it if I want to go for promotion."

I was in full support of Garrett gaining promotion and climbing the hierarchy within the police force. "Which you do," I said.

"Which I do," he agreed.

The only issue I had, which had become a burning but un-askable question, was that the courses and 'emergency' meetings he had to attend all fell at around the same time—just before the full moon. At first, I hadn't realised he was never around during that time, but it slowly dawned upon me, that he wasn't. I had been expecting some excuse to come up this month too, all the while remembering the turret at Blackwood Manor with its scarred panelling and heavy chair with thick iron shackles. Announcing the course had come on cue. I wanted to ask him if the Blackwood curse was lycanthropic and if he was cursed too. I felt sure of the answer, but so far hadn't had the courage to broach it. I remembered the beast who had saved me after I'd passed out in the woods.

A huge arm had pushed beneath my shoulders, and another beneath my thighs, as strong arms had locked me to the beast's chest. As it carried me to Blackwood Manor, I studied it. It was huge, with a thick layer of soft hair that covered a muscular chest and abdomen. Its head was covered in hair but where sharp canines protruded onto its lower lip, its nose, though distorted was more human than wolf-like. And those eyes – darkest amber with long and curling lashes!

I glanced at Garrett, and our eyes met. Amber eyes, complete with long and curling lashes locked onto mine. A tingle of heat began to rise in my cheeks, and I picked up the teapot as a distraction. As I began to pour out the tea, the café doorbell tinkled, and a woman walked in. I could tell from the way she scanned the room, and the clipboard in her hand, that she wasn't here to drink tea or eat cake. She waved at the owner who was busy at the coffee maker then stepped up to the first table. Her voice was low as she bent to speak to the women at the table, and then she held out the clipboard. The first woman took the pen she offered and signed then passed it to her companions. The scene was repeated for each table until she reached ours.

"Good afternoon," she smiled. Broad shouldered and tall, with long dark hair, she towered over us. She looked familiar but I struggled to place her. Light caught her face and highlighted several dark and curling whiskers beneath her chin and more across her top lip. Apart from the whiskers, she was well dressed, with immaculately groomed hair, and perfectly applied makeup. She was attractive in a horse-like and solid way.

We both returned her greeting.

"If I could take a moment of your time, please. I'm asking all locals to sign this petition."

"Oh? What's it about?" Garrett asked.

"The village reputation and the risks of degenerate behaviour damaging our young people."

"Oh?"

"Yes. I don't know if you are aware of it, but a house of ill-repute has been opened in the village."

I sighed. Hrok.

"A house of ill-repute?" Garrett asked.

"Yes! A brothel!" she spat.

"That's the first I've heard of it," Garrett said, casting me a questioning frown.

"It is a harem! A den of iniquity and must be expunged from the village. Think of our children, how their minds will be warped. Think of the husbands tempted into sin! Purity is joy!"

"Purity is joy?"

"Exactly! And without purity there is only filth."

"Right-"

She thrust the clipboard above Garrett's cup as he lifted it towards his mouth. "Please sign this petition. We are going to present it to the Parish Council and have the filth that has infected our village scraped out like a puss-filled boil. Purified!"

"Where is this 'brothel'?" Garrett asked.

"Leodrune House. A man who calls himself Roger Carmichael lives there with six prostitutes."

Garrett cast me a glance.

"They're not prostitutes!" I said in Hrok's defence. "They're sisters living with their brother."

Garrett's eyes widened. I realised my mistake immediately.

"He is fornicating with his sisters! Incest in the village! The very devil has come to visit Haligern!"

"No! I mean ... Not like that! I think they call him brother because he is the leader of their ... cult. But it's not a brothel. More like a ... nunnery or a monastery."

Garrett shook his head, a laugh barely suppressed.

The woman thrust the petition in my face. "Sign!" she demanded. "Help us rid the village of Satan and his whores!"

Chapter Seven

I had been using Aunt Thomasin's cream for several days and noticed a discernible difference. My skin glowed, the redness on my cheeks had gone, and the open pores around my nose had disappeared. In the mirror, even in the harsh light of the kitchen window, I looked a good ten years younger. I opened the shop with a smile and a sense of intense wellbeing which was either a side effect of the cream or a sneaky drop or two of one of my aunts' elixirs. I had come to suspect Aunt Beatrice of adding drops to my tea on a regular basis and began to wonder if she was experimenting on me. She'd given me a particularly sheepish look when that thought had crossed my mind over breakfast after a frisson of energy passed down the back of my throat as I'd swallowed a mouthful of the dark brew.

The logs in the burner were crackling and the shop had warmed before the first customer arrived, the woman who had fallen in the road after speaking to Hrok. I resisted the urge to ask her what he had spoken to her about and helped her choose a gift for her friend's thirtieth birthday. As we walked about the shop choosing items on my recommendation, I realised I had been wrong about two things. She was much younger than me and, in the light, I caught sight of several longer hairs beneath her chin which made me realise that it would be useful to start research on a good hair removal cream. We sold one developed by Aunt Thomasin, but I'd found it ineffective for long term removal. With her gifts wrapped, she left the shop, and it was several minutes before the next customer arrived.

The bell tinkled and I turned from dusting a bottle of dried red clover to see a broad-shouldered and tall blonde woman standing in the doorway. Her cheeks were rosy from the cold.

"Good morning, Mrs. Burchill," I said. Glenda Burchill was a regular customer and often ordered a selection of creams and potions to be made into hampers for friends and relatives.

"Morning, Liv. It's lovely and warm in here."

"The log burner does a wonderful job."

"It's such a wonderful shop. I wish you had a sofa in here and served coffee and cakes. I could sit for hours. It has such an inviting atmosphere."

"Why, thank you! We've tried to make it a welcoming space."

"And you have, but then I've always liked your aunts. They've done so much for the village over the years. Your Aunt Loveday blessed my dad's garden the other day. He swears by it. He says that if she doesn't bless it, then his crops don't grow as well."

"She does have the magic touch," I said.

Mrs. Burchill continued to chat as she moved around the shop, looking at the various ointments, salves, and creams that were on the large Welsh dresser. She chose a cleanser that promised to shrink 'boyles that aflyct the skyne' (Aunt Euphemia's speciality) for her teenage niece who was suffering with pimples, and another (one of Aunt Beatrice's lotions) for 'hard skyne that crackes' for her father. "He has terribly thick skin on his heels," she explained as she placed the jar on the counter. I began to add up the cost.

"My goodness! Look up a minute," she said.

Surprised, I looked up.

"Yes! I thought so."

Suddenly self-conscious under her scrutiny, I placed a hand to my cheek. "What is it?"

"Your skin looks amazing! You're using a new cream, aren't you."

She grasped my chin, turning my head from side to side, inspecting my skin.

"Those open pores have all gone!"

A warm flush rushed to my cheeks.

"Or have you had a chemical peel? Marcia Hepplewhite had one done the year before last, but the effects were nowhere near as good as yours." She released my chin.

Taken aback, I gathered my senses. "It's a new cream-"

"I knew it! Thomasin said that she was trying to improve the last one. I thought that one was very effective, but this ..." She continued to scrutinize my face. "I'll take two jars. It is for sale, isn't it?"

"We haven't launched yet-"

"Do you have some in the back?"

"I nodded."

"Good. Can I have two then, please?"

I nodded, surprised at the intensity of her reaction, then made my way to the back of the shop and the storeroom.

"You really do look years younger, Liv."

"Thanks," I managed, still self-conscious under her intense gaze.

"I tell you what, we're down a demonstrator for this week's meeting at the W. I. Will you come along? You can use it to launch your cream. What do you say?"

"Well, I-"

"Now, don't say no! You'll be doing me a huge favour. We've got an opening for our next slot – the presenter cancelled so I guess we'll have to learn how to sew sock monkeys another time," she said with a raise of a brow and a wry smile. "We have some wonderful demonstrations but sometimes ... well, they leave a lot to be desired. There will be tea and coffee, or wine if you prefer ... It will be good for business. I've been using your creams for a while and spread the word, but my goodness, Liv, your skin looks beautiful, and the difference is so ... obvious. I came in the other day and noticed but came back to check."

"Check?"

"Yes, well, after Martha's special face mask ... don't get me wrong! I think Martha is wonderful, but her face mask ... it worked so well and then it didn't, but your cream, it looks like it works to me."

I managed a smile. "I've definitely noticed a difference in my skin tone."

"Yes, and that saggy bit beneath your chin doesn't look so ... saggy, anymore," she beamed.

I touched the soft skin beneath my chin, there was a definite sag of jowly skin although it did feel firmer. "Thanks," I managed. "I guess I could. What would I have to do?"

"Oh, just turn up and take them through your cleansing and moisturising routine. I'll be your model, if you like, to make things easy."

I managed a laugh. "Okay, I'll do it."

"Excellent. Bring some of your other products too. We can set up a table for you. The ladies love things to nose through after they've had their tea and cake. You'll make sales, I'm sure of it. Bring plenty of your new cream too. It will fly off the shelves!"

"It sounds great, thank you."

"Good. So that's settled then. Bring all your lotions and potions over to the Old School House on Wednesday. The ladies arrive at six pm so you may like to come over a little earlier."

"Wednesday? But that's tomorrow."

"It is," she beamed. "See you then." She turned and waved without waiting for a reply and I watched her leave as the bell tinkled and she disappeared through the door.

A dandelion headed fairy buzzed up from beneath the counter, chittered, swooped to my shoulder then fluttered beneath my chin. I felt a sharp prick, heard another chitter followed by a chuckling laugh, and then the creature swooped across to the grandfather clock and disappeared inside, plucked hair held aloft like a trophy.

"I heard that!" I chided as I rubbed the flesh beneath my chin. The buzz within the grandfather clock was drowned out by tiny cackling chitters.

Chapter Eight

Wednesday evening came, and I stayed at the shop rather than going home and used the time to prepare for the demonstration. I had decided to take up Glenda Burchill's offer of being my model and would be going through my cleansing and moisturising routine as suggested. There were a number of Haligern Apothecary products that I used at home, and I packed samples of them all to be made available for purchase after the demonstration. I also packed a box of other creams and lotions. Aunt Euphemia wanted me to take some of her winter balm, a collection of winter flower and berry inspired creams made for the coming months of cold and harsh winds. They were creamy, smelled delicious, and gave a warm tingle when they were smeared across the skin. The warmth lasted for nearly ten minutes and was wonderfully soothing. I packed the entire collection along with several of Aunt Thomasin's calmatives, and Aunt Beatrice's bath oils. I decided against promoting our in-development line of creams for the tightening and/or moistening of ladies' nether regions. Research was ongoing but I was planning to quietly add the results to our line of menopausal products rather than suffer the uncomfortable experience of launching them individually. An open evening for creams for that part of a woman's anatomy would garner very few guests, despite genuine interest, and I felt sure that a gentle mention of their existence to our existing clients, perhaps in a carefully worded email about new products, would be the best way forward.

I arrived at the Victorian school house, where the Haligern branch of the Women's Institute was held once a month, fifteen minutes early. As I pulled into the carpark a tall woman with dark brown hair was fumbling in her bag at the school's back door. She had her back to me until I reached her side just as the key was turned in the lock and the door swung open.

She eyed me with surprise.

"Sorry! I didn't mean to startle you," I said as she threw me a momentary glare.

In the moment our eyes met, I recognised her as the rabid, petition-bearing woman from the café. She was familiar, but I still couldn't remember her name or place her within my memory.

Pursed lips dissolved beneath a forced smile. "Can I help you?"

"I'm here to give a demonstration."

"Sock monkeys?"

Had the sock monkey lady decided to give a demonstration after all? I began to feel a little foolish. Glenda hadn't confirmed that I was booked in to give the evening's presentation. Did she even have the authority to do that? "No, sorry. Have I got the wrong night?" I asked, desperately trying to find a reason to be standing at the schoolroom door without looking foolish.

"The Women's Institute is meeting here tonight. Are you demonstrating?" she asked with a glance at the stack of boxes in my arms.

"I think so, although I'm not the sock monkey lady."

Relief seemed to pass across her face. "Of course! You're Livitha from Haligern Apothecary. Don't worry. I'm not as scatty as I seem. Glenda did tell me."

Relief passed through me. "Oh, good!"

Her eyes narrowed momentarily. "I'm Priscilla, by the way."

I smiled by way of return, unsure what to say. I should know this woman. She was local, had perhaps been into the shop, and I didn't want to cause offence by making it obvious I hadn't remembered her name.

We stepped through the door and the woman led me through to the hall. Along one wall there were stacks of chairs whilst on the opposite side there were a stack of tables. Priscilla helped lift two tables, instructed me to set them out as I pleased, then marched to the kitchen to fill up the kettles and turn the heating on. The room was chilly, and I hoped that it would warm up before I began my demonstration.

I moved the tables into the positions that Priscilla had suggested and placed two chairs beneath the one I would use to demonstrate from. On the other, I spread a pristine cloth prettily embroidered with flowers and insects around its border. I had brought along one of our display shelves and fetched it in from the car. It resembled the top of a Welsh dresser and had been painted black. I stacked it with jars and bottles in an artful display, and then focused on the table's surface. Here I stacked Aunt Thomasin's wonder cream in a pyramid of glistening jars. I had brought along a couple of vintage sweet jars and filled them with prettily coloured soaps, also made by my aunts. By the time I had finished, and stood back to observe my efforts, the members were filtering in through the door.

"Ooh! This looks interesting!"

"I thought we were sewing sock monkeys tonight," one of the women said as she reached my side. I recognised her as a regular at the shop.

"Janice said she cancelled. Can't say I'm sorry and this does look more interesting," another woman said as she scanned the shelves with their coloured glass bottles and jars of shimmering oils. She smiled at me as our eyes met. I didn't recognise her, but she seemed to be a friend of the lady that I did recognise.

As more women arrived, the room filled with chatter and laughter. I recognised some of the women, but others were unfamiliar. Among them were several customers. I had thought I would recognise all of the women but was pleased to be wrong. New faces meant potential new customers for the apothecary and once a customer bought one of our products, they would often come back for more and try other products too.

I caught Priscilla watching me on a couple of occasions, and several of the other women seemed particularly interested in me too. I put this down to me being the demonstrator and therefore the focus of attention for that night's entertainment. There were some though, whose attention seemed to be hostile. Two women in particular, seated directly opposite the demonstration table, talked between themselves whilst glancing my way, their lips pursed beneath disapproving frowns.

If the wind changes, you'll stay that way! I pressed my lips together and made a pretence of continuing to organise the bottles. *You sour-faced old bags.*

'Not everyone in the village likes us, dear', I remembered Aunt Loveday saying after a trip to the local butcher had turned sour. 'You mean they disapprove of us,' I had countered. 'Well, some of the ladies are of a devout mindset,' she had replied. The woman with the 'devout mindset' had passed me in the street. With her carefully rolled and blow-dried hair set with lacquer, she had looked like the quintessentially respectable housewife in her fitted jacket and pleated below-the-knee skirt, but she had narrowed her eyes as she approached me on the path, then puckered her mouth before spitting at my feet. Shocked at her behaviour, I assumed she had some sort of mental illness, but another lady stepped by my side and told me to take no notice of her. 'There's some here with long memories, Liv,' she had said. 'And some that don't like anyone who is different.' That my family was different from the rest of the villagers had been obvious from my early childhood, but the incident with the spitting woman had been the first time any animosity had been shown towards me by an adult.

As the women on the front row continued to cast evil eyes towards me, I busied myself arranging the products I would need, and was relieved when Glenda arrived. Unlike the scowling women, she beamed as she approached the table. After calling for a bowl of warm water, she turned to the gathered crowd. There were now three rows of seats with a central aisle giving access to the back of the room. All were filled and I stood beside Glenda looking into a sea of faces.

"Good evening, ladies," she began. "I know you're all terribly disappointed that Ursula can't be with us tonight to show us how to sew sock puppets," she said in a tone of forced enthusiasm met by chuntering and some laughter, "but I am extremely excited, and we are most fortunate, to have Livitha Erikson from Haligern Apothecary with us tonight. Let's give her a Haligern Homemakers welcome!"

This was met by loud applause and as I looked out across the women I picked up on waves of uplifting energy. They seemed genuinely pleased and, apart from a few sour-faced women here and there, their smiles were broad and welcoming. I breathed a sigh of relief; I was accepted.

"Now, there's a particular reason that I invited Livitha to come along tonight, and I don't think she'll mind me saying this, but I have noticed a wonderful improvement in her skin." The women focused their attention on my face. I returned their inquisitive stares with a smile, holding down the wave of self-consciousness that threatened to overwhelm me. "And she tells me that it is because of a new cream the Haligern Cottage sisters have developed."

To my surprise, she grabbed my hand. "Come and show them, Livitha."

Before I had a chance to reply, she led me to the rows of women, parading me up and down the central aisle to exclamations of 'Ooh!' and 'Oh, yes! I can see a difference', along with, 'Not so baggy under the eyes', as well as the gut-twisting, 'And that 'tache isn't so obvious!'

Mortified at being paraded like a prize cow whilst being bombarded with intensely personal comments, I was relieved to be guided back to the demonstration table. Glenda retained control of proceedings, instructing me to begin with a cleanse of her face and to explain what I was doing as I went along.

I acquiesced without resistance; this was her turf, not mine.

One of the women left her seat, mobile in hand, and thrust it into Glenda's face. "Let's get before and after shots!" she said whilst taking photographs.

"Just don't upload them, Kate," Glenda warned as I wiped at her cheek with a warm cloth. She moved her head to face the camera. The camera clicked. "Got it?" she asked.

"Yep!" replied Kate whilst scrolling through the photographs. She turned the screen to Glenda. "Let's hope it does as good a job on your 'tache as it did on Liv's," she said with a grunt of laughter.

Glenda rolled her eyes in good humour. "I'll buy you a tub for your birthday, Kate!"

Both women cackled and Kate remained close, now filming the event. I took a deep breath, my nerves on edge. As I finished the cleansing and began to explain the ingredients – sans the magical infusions – and properties of the cleansing fluid, I relaxed. With the pot of anti-ageing wonder cream in hand, the women grew silent and watched as I dotted it across Glenda's cheeks, forehead, chin, and nose, then worked it in with gentle, massaging, strokes. Beneath my hands, Glenda's energy changed to one of deep relaxation and I felt the waves of wellbeing waft from her. It was a new sensation to me. I had only ever moisturised my own face. I finished with a gentle rub in tiny circles at her temple.

She opened her eyes. "Oh, my! That was nice. So soothing. Thank you, Livitha."

"My pleasure," I said.

"I feel younger already," she laughed.

"Has it worked?" one woman asked.

"Give it a chance," another retorted. "Anti-ageing creams take weeks."

"She looks better already."

"That's because she's so relaxed."

"Yes, but that redness on her skin has already calmed down."

"And she's not so saggy under the chin."

"It can't possibly work that quickly. The only thing that does that is Botox or fillers!" declared Valerie Hodgkin, a bleached blonde complete with fake tan whose pouting lips looked as though they'd been given industrial-level help to look full and plump.

I passed Glenda the hand mirror. She held it up, squinting against the light until she moved into position. "Well!" A broad smile broke across her face. "I swear I already see the difference."

"It'll just be some particles they've put in it that blur your vision," declared Valerie. "They reflect the light so that your skin looks smoother and less wrinkled to other people."

"There are no light-reflective particles in our creams, Mrs. Hodgkin," I said, beginning to feel defensive. "We only use natural products, most of them grown at Haligern Cottage."

The woman's overly inflated lips pouted even more as she pursed them.

"Turn to me, Glenda," Kate demanded. "Get in the exact position you were in when I took the first photos. We'll compare them."

Glenda turned and Kate took another photograph, then scrolled and pressed the buttons on her phone. "Wow!" she said then held up her phone. "The difference is real! You can see it when you compare the photographs."

The room erupted with chatter and the scraping of chairs as the women surged to the front. We were suddenly surrounded as more than two dozen women scrutinized Glenda's face whilst the others flocked around Kate and her photographs.

After the initial flurry, the flock moved across to the table where I had arranged the creams. Within a minute every jar of the anti-ageing cream had been taken.

"I'd say that's what you call success!" beamed Glenda. I returned her smile, noticing the improvement in her skin. The redness was reduced and the bags beneath her eyes were less visible. She had a youthful glow that no injection of fillers or Botox could create.

As I wrapped jars in tissue paper, placed them in bags, and took the ladies' money, I felt a wave of cold energy rise over the crowd and stroke me with its fingers. I shivered, looked out across the room, and was instantly drawn to a gaggle of women deep in conversation. Their collective energy was cold, damp, and unpleasant. They glanced towards me, noticed me watching, then returned to chatting among themselves. That they were talking about me was obvious. Among them was Priscilla Dedman, the woman I hadn't been able to remember and who turned out to be the Chairman of Haligern's branch of the Women's Institute, the Haligern Homemakers. Hazily opaque memories of school shifted across my mind.

Chapter Nine

With all the products sold, bar a few salves, I took the cup of tea offered to me by one of the beaming women who assured me she was going to try out the cream tonight. Cup in hand, I joined the throng of women, gravitating to a small group that included some well-known customers. I was met with a barrage of questions that I happily answered and was pleased that they all seemed genuinely interested in our products and promised to visit the shop soon. I pondered whether to mention the nether region tightening and moistening creams I was working on but decided against broaching the subject.

"And have you seen them?" a shrill voice cut through my thoughts. "They are brazen about it!"

"My George thinks it's a knocking shop!"

"Such a beautiful house too! One of the best in the village."

"They're bringing the village into disrepute. Kelly was complaining that if news got out that we had a brothel – excuse my French – in the village, it could turn people away and you know how hard she's worked on getting that B&B up and running."

"It's so seedy."

"The B&B's lovely!"

"No, the brothel. So gross!"

The group of women that surrounded me, turned their attention to the gossiping women.

"What are they talking about?" I asked with a sinking sensation in my gut. It was a rhetorical question. I knew who the focus of their vitriol was directed against.

"Roger Carmichael and his wives," said Glenda with authority.

"Wives! How can a man have six wives, Glenda? That's illegal—at least in this country, although it's going to the dogs so who knows ..."

"Well, legally, I don't believe they are wives-"

"Concubines!" The voice was loud, cutting through the noise in the room. "Whores!" Priscilla had zoned in on our conversation and turned her attention our way. "Roger Carmichael has created his very own harem and it is sinful!" Her eyes blazed and she looked to her companion, a tall woman with white-blonde hair. I hadn't noticed her before, but now it was hard not to stare. Statuesque, she could have been Angelina Jolie's twin sister, but for the dark hair. Her green eyes caught mine, the emerald green seeming to flicker as it caught the overhead light.

"That's right, Priscilla," she agreed. "They are living in dreadful sin. They are unclean. Purity, after all, is joy." The words flowed with honied tones.

Glenda sighed beside me. "Here we go," she said in a low voice. "Another lecture."

"This village is sinking into degeneracy," the woman continued. "And it will infect us all. Ladies," she said, casting a slow look around the room, "think of your husbands." The women began to mutter. "Think of the fantasies that the harem of filth will arouse in your men."

"They'll never get my man!" a woman shouted from the back.

"I've heard they offer a free turn to get them hooked."

I wanted to dig a little further; did they realise the true nature of Roger Carmichael and his concubines? "Where is this house?" I asked.

"Roger Carmichael is renting Leodrune House from the Slawston family," Glenda explained. "The gossip is that the women who live with him are his lovers, but Priscilla is certain that the women are prostitutes and she's on a mission to get the house shut down, along with her new best friend." She gestured to the tall blonde. "It's all rubbish, of course."

"Who is her new best friend?"

"She's called Prudence. And she's just as crazy as Priscilla, if you ask me. Runs a purity club, but it's just a money-grabbing cult."

"Do they say anything else? About Roger?"

"Other than that the village has its very own Hugh Heffner in residence complete with Playboy bunnies? Not that I know of."

"I hope all of you ladies have signed the petition." Priscilla scanned the room. "I have left it on the table for you to sign if you haven't." She spoke with a menacing glare, and I had to agree with Glenda that she was a touch crazy, or at the very least, obsessed.

It was a relief to know that the villagers were ignorant of Hrok's true nature, but from Priscilla's condemnation and fiery words, there already seemed to be a witch hunt underway. I determined to offer a different explanation to the group's living arrangements.

"Perhaps they're just friends, or even relatives," I suggested.

Priscilla turned on me, a flash of rage in her eyes. "Friends!" she spat, taking steps towards me. "Relatives!"

"Well, it's possible," I said taking a step back as she bore down upon me.

Hard eyes, dark and sludgy brown, bored into me. "The man has been seen cavorting in his hot tub with all the women," she said. "They have sauntered through the village making no attempt to hide their lasciviousness."

"What does 'lasciviousness' mean?" a woman behind me asked.

"It means being sexual," Glenda replied in a staged whisper.

"Oh! I see. I did see him kissing one in the lane. And he had his hand on the other one's bum," she said.

"See!" seethed Priscilla. "See!"

She seemed demented and a wicked thought crossed my mind. "Does your husband fancy them, Priscilla?" Tweaking Priscilla was a mistake. She rose to her full height, scowled down at me and, without warning, grabbed my hair.

"Agh!" I cried as I was tugged forward.

"Priscilla!" I heard Glenda shout. "Don't!"

The room became silent and then erupted with noise. As fingers gripped my hair like steel prongs, and my head was pulled towards the wide boards of the old schoolroom, I heard a chant I had not heard since school.

"Fight! Fight! Fight!"

How had I forgotten? Priscilla Dedman, Chairman of Haligern's Women's Institute, was my childhood bully.

"Fight! Fight! Fight!" The cluster of middle-aged women chanted as they circled like vultures, their voices transforming to girlish shouts. "Fight! Fight! Fight!"

I was back in the playground, Priscilla Dedman's hand was attached to my plaits, and she was pulling me down towards the tarmac. A white square with the number four was directly beneath me, the hopscotch grid I had just begun to draw.

"She was drawing a pentagram," Priscilla shouted. "She's a witch!"

"Witch! Witch! Witch!" the girls chanted.

"It's ... for ... hopscotch," I managed as I grabbed the root of my plaits to stop the pain.

"She's a witch and she put a spell on her dad, and he disappeared with a puff of smoke!" Another girl shouted.

"And she turned her mum into a toad!" another squealed with vicious delight.

My heart broke for the millionth time. I had never known either of my parents. They had died when I was a baby. My aunts tried to fill the gap, but the pain of their absence was keen.

"They're all witches! My mum said they cast spells and dance naked at midnight in the woods. She's seen them."

"That's a lie!" I screamed as pain and rage overcame me.

The women's voices returned, and I felt pressure on my shoulders as my hair was released. The pain on my scalp had been intense and lingered as I was pulled away from my attacker. Priscilla lay on the floor, her eyes focused on the ceiling, staring and wide.

"What happened?" I asked.

"You ... I'm not sure, but one minute she was attacking you, then the lights went out and Priscilla was on the floor."

"She's not dead, is she?" I asked too stunned to think straight.

"Not by the looks of it," Glenda said as Priscilla turned her head, confusion passing over dazed eyes.

"I'm so sorry, Livitha." Glenda slipped an arm across my shoulder.

Still in shock, I could think of no sensible reply.

"I think you hit a nerve. If her husband's been to Roger's house, it wouldn't be the first time he's strayed."

"He's been unfaithful?" I managed.

"I don't know about recently, but I do know he had an affair with a woman from work. Priscilla nearly divorced him, but the thought of losing her house and fancy cars put a stop to it."

Priscilla was helped to stand then walked across to a chair. She threw me a scathing glance.

"Looks like she's got it in for you, Liv, but then again, she always has."

"I know. I'd forgotten all about it until she grabbed my hair." I touched fingers to my head, the tips sparked with the remnants of magick I must have used to defend myself. "I think I'll pack up and go home."

Chapter Ten

The following morning, I woke with a dry mouth, pain throbbing in my head, and Lucifer's needling claws piercing my thigh.

"It's time to rise, Livitha," he said.

I grunted in return and laid with eyes open, adjusting to the dark. "It's early I grumbled." Memories of last night's brawl seeped into my waking mind and the mortification that had smothered me as Priscilla Dedman pulled me around the schoolroom by the hair was even more keen this morning. All the women had seen what she had done. The same women who had chanted in the playground when she attacked me then, had chanted in the schoolroom, their eyes just as greedy for pain as they ever were.

"No, it's time to rise," he repeated. "November always has dark mornings. The fire is laid, and your aunts are expecting you to break your fast with them."

"They hate me." Self-pity oozed with my words.

"What's new?" he asked.

"Where were you when I needed you?" I complained then reached over to the lamp and switched on the bedside light.

Lucifer hissed, sat in frigid attention, then relaxed and began licking a paw. "What a frightful sight," he said.

"Thanks! I feel bad enough as it is without your commentary, Lucifer." I eased myself to sit up then swung my legs over the bed. Each muscle in my body ached.

"Well, you do look monstrous!"

"Blah! Blah! Blah! If you're going to go on about how I have hairs beneath my chin and on my top lip, then I'm just not going to take the bait today."

"I suggest that you look in the mirror, Mistress, before you disparage me for another second." He jumped off the bed and sauntered to the door, tail held high. He gave it a final irritated flick, then slipped through the gap and out onto the hallway. "Your aunts are waiting. The time for being slothful should have come to an end in your teenage years."

I glanced at the clock. "It's only seven o'clock. That's hardly being slothful."

"Pah!" he said from the landing. "Your aunts arose at five of the clock."

I listened as he padded down the stairs, resisting the temptation to argue, and made my way into the bathroom. Lucifer had a habit of commenting on my appearance. Most of the time he did it to be annoying, at others to be spiteful and, on rare occasions, when there was an issue. I knew that Aunt Thomasin's cream had worked wonders on my skin, reducing the spidery broken veins and open pores that came with ageing, so assumed he was just trying to be annoying. My head pounded, every follicle on my scalp seeming to remember Priscilla's abuse.

In the bathroom, I switched on the light, flinched at the pain it caused across my eyes, and squinted as I approached the mirror.

There was no need to open the curtains for extra light, or to lean in close to peer at my skin in the mirror, for me to see that Lucifer was right. I looked monstrous. For several moments I stood mesmerised by my reflection, too shocked to move or react. The woman staring back at me was wild haired and dishevelled, but it was the dark bruising and swollen eye that made her look crazy. Her lips were also swollen and a split at one side was crusted with blood.

I stepped a little closer to the mirror, closing and opening my eyes to look again, hoping that the reflection was a hallucination. The beaten woman stared back.

"What happened?" My memories of last night were hazy, as though seen through a fog. I remembered that Priscilla had pulled my hair, forcing me down towards the floor, but the evidence on my face showed that she had punched me too, possibly even given me a boot whilst I was down. I touched a gentle finger to my lip. It felt hard, swollen, and crusted around the split. I ran a tongue along my teeth. All were present. I breathed a sigh of relief. With my head throbbing, and the shame of mortification making me feel grubby, I showered. The warmth was soothing and within half an hour I was ready to face my aunts. None had been home when I returned from the Women's Institute, and I had fallen into bed without seeing them. I made my way downstairs with trepidation, knowing that my appearance would cause great shock. I was fifty years old and had been beaten up on a night out. Shame slithered over me.

"Ah, Livitha," Aunt Beatrice said as I pushed the kitchen door open. "Good morning. Sit down. I have just made a fresh pot of tea and there's porridge in the pot. Do you want stewed apples or peaches with it?"

"Peaches," I mumbled as I walked to the table. Aunt Beatrice's back was turned to me as I sat down, and I was thankful that the room was empty bar Renweard sat curled on his cushion before the fire. Benny squawked from the curtain pole with a beady eye trained on me.

I waited at the table as Aunt Beatrice reached for a fresh cup and saucer. She placed them on the table then returned to the counter for the tea pot. Surprised that she hadn't noticed my face, I poured myself a cup of tea. She returned with a bowl of porridge topped by a generous serving of steamed peaches. She placed a pot of honey beside me.

"The peaches are sweet enough, but you may want to add some honey to help with the shock although I'll put several drops of your aunt's strongest calmative into the teapot. We're all aquiver in the house." She lifted the teapot lid and allowed several drops of the elixir to fall then added a splash more. She caught my eye as she replaced the lid. A momentary flicker of silver sparks swimming in her iris was the only sign she had noticed my bruised and swollen face. "And so close to the Night!" She moved back to the kitchen sink whilst muttering under her breath.

After pouring myself a cup of tea, I took a generous mouthful and swallowed. The elixir was strong and left a bitterness on my tongue but as it slid down my throat, the warmth of its power began to spread to every capillary in my body. I relaxed in my chair, a little heavy eyed, but with the pain in my scalp receding. The sense of shame lifted a little too. Without speaking, I began to eat my porridge.

In the next minutes, my other aunts entered the room. The energy in the kitchen changed and although I sat within a bubble of calm, sparks crackled in the air above them.

"Look at her!" Aunt Thomasin said. "This is all my fault."

"Don't be ridiculous!" chided Aunt Euphemia.

Aunt Loveday shook her head. "Of course it's not your fault, Thomasin."

"It's Hetty Yikkar's fault!" The pitch of Aunt Beatrice's voice was an octave short of hysteria.

"Hsst!"

Aunt Beatrice clapped a hand to her mouth. "It is she who shall not be named! It is her!" she said with a dramatic glance into the corners of the room.

Aunt Loveday took a deep breath. "Beatrice, have you laced the tea as I instructed?"

She nodded.

"Then pour yourself some and sit down. Drink it before you infect the house with your fearmongering."

Aunt Beatrice pulled out a seat. Aunt Euphemia poured her a cup of tea and placed it before her. She drank it in two large gulps.

"It's my fault," I said, the soporific effect of the tea making me slur my words.

"I think Bea has overdone it with the calmative, sister," said Aunt Thomasin. "She's drunk with it."

Aunt Loveday placed a hand on my shoulder. The pressure was reassuring, and I felt the energy from it rush through my body. The mortification that had laid over me like a damp pall, lifted.

"She is fine," Aunt Loveday said. "Just in shock."

"I am not surprised. And look at her face."

"It is a mess."

"Is that a footprint?" Aunt Thomasin leant down and took my chin in her hands. "It is. Oh, Loveday. I fear we are on the cusp of something terrible."

"And so close to the Night!" Aunt Beatrice repeated in a doom-laden voice.

"Now, now, sisters. We must not allow this hysterical energy to infect us. We have survived hundreds of these nights."

"Since 1487," said Beatrice. "Oh, I remember it as though it were yesterday. The screams. The smell of burning flesh!"

Aunt Thomasin groaned and Aunt Euphemia clasped her silver bangle. Even Aunt Loveday swayed a little.

"Do you remember, sisters? The night Het- ... she was burned at the stake!"

"Of course we do."

"I tell you, I feel it in my bones, we are the edge of the abyss!"

"For once I wish that Grimlock would arrive with an assignment for her. I would gladly listen to her crowing about it rather than suffer this!" said Aunt Euphemia.

"Also, I," agreed Aunt Thomasin.

"Well, he hasn't and likely won't, at least not until after the Night," Loveday said. She grew quiet then said, "I shall refresh the protection around Haligern. Sisters, I think that we should do it together."

"You feel it too, then?"

"I hate to admit it, but Beatrice may be right. There is definitely something in the air. I have felt it in the village these past days."

"There's a petition against Hrok and the Slawston sisters," I said. "The village seems to have taken against them."

The air crackled above Aunt Loveday, embers sparking against the rafters.

"And then there's that cult Mrs. Driscoll told us about. 'Purity is joy.'"

"And Hrok was making a nuisance of himself in the village. He kept asking women the time until he nearly got beaten up by one of the husbands," I said. "And I think he used magick against them because the husband knocked into a post and then the wife fell off the pavement, but it looked as though she had been pushed, but Hrok was nowhere to be seen and he did look shocked," I said, and then drew breath.

The room grew quiet.

"Was there anyone else around at the time?"

"I watched with Garrett from the shop window and customers at the café were watching from their tables at the window."

"Anyone else?"

I shook my head. "I didn't see anyone else. The fairies were going crazy though."

"What are we going to do?" asked Aunt Euphemia.

"About Hrok? Nothing," stated Aunt Loveday.

"What about the woman that attacked Livitha?"

"We should report her to the police for assault," declared Aunt Beatrice.

Aunt Loveday shook her head. "I think we should continue as normal. I know that it is hard, but you must go into the shop this morning, Livitha. I have cream that will help take down the swelling and bruising. We must show no fear. If they get a whiff of that, they will take it as weakness and that is when the real trouble begins."

Chapter Eleven

Aunt Thomasin insisted on applying salve to my swollen
face herself. Her energy crackled as she tutted and gently
smoothed cream across the purpling skin around my eye. She
applied a different ointment to my split lip and then another
beneath my eye to help with the puffiness. "There," she
declared. "It does look sore, but the swelling is already going
down and the bruising is less fierce." She passed me a mirror.
The woman reflected back looked a little sorry for herself, but
her swollen eye was less colourful and more open. The boot
mark on her cheek had faded and the split on her lip had
almost healed.

"Thank you," I said.

She placed a hand on my shoulder. "We have all faced
adversity over the centuries. There's not one among us who
hasn't been attacked by one of them." She managed a smile that
was both pitying and encouraging. "It's far worse when one of
our own tries to harm us. They can do real damage."

"Then I hope no one takes against me."

"Oh, you'll know how to deal with them when they do,
Livitha. I'm confident of that. You've managed wonderfully
well so far. Turning Millicent into a goat just as the dragon
from your bangle came to your defence was inspired. A

moment of pure joy for us. She was poisonous, Livitha, and far too powerful for the good of the covens."

I felt buoyed by her pep talk. "Thanks, Aunt Thomasin."

With my energy lifted, I picked up another box of the anti-ageing cream from the table and made my way to the shop. After the humiliation at the Women's Institute, I was dreading facing the customers. I had no doubt that there would be rubber necking villagers, curious to see the woman beaten up by the Chairman, Priscilla Dedman. Old emotions rode me as I motored along the winding lanes from Haligern Cottage and I was plunged back to my schooldays, standing in the playground waiting for the bell to ring, trying not to attract the notice of the gaggle of spite-filled girls clustering around Priscilla. Then, as now, I had a blackened eye from her punch.

"You won't do it again!" Hate churned within me and it was surprisingly satisfying. "I'll show you! I'm not going to hide and scurry away beneath a rock like you want me to."

Embrace who you are. Ancient voices repeated in my mind. *Rise into your power.*

"I will!" I said, then crunched the gears into third as I took a bend too quickly. I righted the car, only narrowly missing the verge, took a breath and berated myself for becoming so agitated. Priscilla had gotten under my skin, but it wasn't until later that I would realise by just how much.

I arrived half an hour before the shop was set to open and locked the door behind me then busied myself preparing the log burner, boiling the kettle for a cup of tea, and scanning the shelves for any obvious gaps that would need restocking.

With elixir infused tea steaming on the counter in my favourite bone china cup and saucer, I checked for any orders, sipping the liquid and enjoying the soothing sensation. Several shoppers passed by, stopped to look inside, then continued along the path. "That's fine," I said as they disappeared. "Take a look. Rubberneck all you want. I'm here and always will be, whether you like it or not."

The fairies fluttered within the grandfather clock, their chittering punctuated with high pitched squeaks, but they made no appearance.

I put another dropper of elixir in my cup and drank the remaining tea in one gulp. Warmth spread through me, and I sighed as the peaceful sensation radiated out from my belly, soothing my fraught nerves.

By ten o'clock, I was ready to open the door and strode across the room. The calmative had worked but there remained an underlying unease. I flipped the sign to open and glanced either side of the street. There were a number of shoppers visiting the greengrocer and the butcher and several women sat in the window of the café. A couple caught sight of me watching. I raised my hand to make a defiant wave, but decided against it and instead fetched a cloth from beneath the counter and began to dust the glass jars and shelves. Several minutes passed before the bell above the door tinkled and a customer stepped inside.

Wearing a scarf over her head and a pair of dark sunglasses over her eyes, her face was barely visible. She seemed familiar and I recognised her as soon as she spoke—Keira Milton, a regular customer. She seemed on edge and stepped up to the counter with a furtive glance out of the windows.

"Are you alright, Keira?" I asked. The only part of her face that was visible was her forehead and tip of her nose, her chin and cheeks being covered by the scarf.

She nodded then removed her glasses. The whites were bloodshot and her eyelids puffy. She had been crying. My own wounds were forgotten.

"Keira, what's wrong?"

Her eyes locked to mine. "Oh, Liv. Something terrible has happened. I don't know what to do. I thought about going to the doctor but ..."

There was an undeniable flicker of fear in her eyes, and her energy was defensive. The scarf began to slip, and she immediately held it to her face.

I grew concerned. Keira had been at the demonstration last night and purchased several different lotions including the new cream. Had there been a reaction? "Is there something wrong with your skin?" I asked with the first flickering of a churning stomach.

She nodded then broke my gaze and looked at the shelves behind me. She lowered the scarf.

I gasped.

Her eyes caught mine for a fleeting second then her face crumpled, and she hid it behind the fabric.

I took a few seconds to gather my senses then asked her to show me her face.

Keira's top lip was covered in dark, long and wispy hairs, but it was at the side of her mouth and at the tip of her chin that they became thick and straggling. They resembled the beard sported by Old Mawde. I glanced at her eyes and then at her head. The pupils were still round without hint of lozenge shape and the scarf sat flat against her hair with no sign of horns protruding. I gave an inward sigh; she hadn't been hexed by a curse, at least not one that would turn her into a goat.

"That is ..." I struggled to find words.

"Horrendous! I know! I don't know what to do. My face is hideous! I shaved it off last night when Frank noticed a few hairs beneath my chin, but this morning it was ..." she sobbed. "Like this!" She thrust her chin out making the dangling beard wave.

I swallowed. "When did it ... they, start growing?" I asked with trepidation.

"I don't know. I didn't notice until after Frank had pointed it out, but you can't miss it anymore!" Her voice was on the verge of hysteria. "And it's not just my face! It's on my chest too." She began to sob.

"Come with me into the back. I'll make you a cup of tea and we can figure out what to do."

I locked the front door and flipped the sign to 'Closed' then led her to the back, sitting her beside the log burner which was throwing out a gentle heat. I made tea, infused it with several drops of the calmative, with an extra one for myself, then sat with her as she drank the brew.

As her sobbing eased and she wiped at her nose with a tissue, I scanned her face. The straggling beard was at least five inches long; a miraculous overnight growth. I touched my own chin. There was no sign of hair. Was it possible that the cream had caused the reaction? I had been the guinea pig, but I wasn't a 'normie' as Aunt Beatrice now called the villagers. I had magical powers. My genetic heritage was completely different from theirs. Did that make a difference?

"I've always loved coming in your shop, Liv. And your aunts do wonders for the village, but last night ... the cream ... could it have done this?" She looked at me with imploring eyes.

"I've been using it myself," I said. "And haven't had that kind of reaction."

"But there's nothing else different! I've trawled my mind for anything that could have caused this. But I've not eaten anything different. I'm not on any medication. The only thing ..." She threw me an apologetic glance. "Is your cream."

Mesmerised by the wispy whiskers as they moved up and down with her mouth, I struggled to reply. "I can't think that it would be the cream. We tested it and ... there's nothing in it that would cause hair growth."

Her lips thinned beneath the whiskers. "Well ... I want help!"

"Yes! Yes, of course you do," I said and offered to fill her cup with more tea.

She accepted and took a sip.

"I'll do what I can," I promised. "There may be something in the shop that will help. Otherwise, I'll talk to my aunts and see what they can advise."

"Thank you," she said and eased back in the chair.

The tea was having the desired effect and I left her nursing the cup whilst I checked the shelves for anything that promised hair reduction. There were several pots of a lotion Aunt Thomasin had made but it hadn't been very effective on my own problematic facial hair so I wasn't confident that it would work. I placed one in a bag anyway.

"Try this after you ... remove it. It may help, but in the meantime, I'm going to talk to my aunts and see if we can discover what's causing the growth and what we can do to help," I reassured her.

She nodded. "Thank you, Liv. I knew you'd help. You always do."

With her eyelids a little heavy, she replaced the scarf over her head, put her sunglasses back on, and left the shop.

Chapter Twelve

On the way over in the car, I had determined to be brazen, and not only open the shop but visit the café for my lunch too. As the clock chimed noon, I locked the shop and walked across the road.

The window was already filled with customers sipping tea and biting into sandwiches and, as I crossed the road, I noticed the ladies in the café watching my progress. I also noticed Hrok. He was standing further down the road, close to the entrance to the village hall. A woman stepped out of the doors. Dressed in leggings that showed off her slim figure, she stopped as he approached her. She smiled then held out her wrist. Hrok returned her smile then attempted to continue the conversation. Not wanting to gawp at the pair, I stepped into the café and made a mental note to visit Hrok. He was up to something, and I doubted it had anything to do with an obsession about time.

I sat at the same table I'd shared with Garrett and waited for the waitress to arrive. She had been surly towards me then, narrowing her eyes as she confirmed I worked at the apothecary, and my stomach did a watery flip as I noticed her glare from across the room. Determined to show no sign of weakness, I took the menu and scanned it. I would have a panini with brie and red onion chutney along with a pot of Earl Grey tea. The woman approached my table.

"Are you ready to order?" she asked with a sharp tone.

Aggressive! "Yes, I am," I replied in a sickly-sweet tone that verged on passive aggressive. "I'd like-" I stalled with all thoughts of melted brie gone. The woman had straggling hairs beneath her chin and there was curly growth beside her ears. Her eyebrows also seemed to be thicker and longer than the other day. I forced myself to stare at the menu, my mind whirring. She had been at the demonstration last night. I remembered her looking across at me from the pack of scowling women that had surrounded Priscilla before the attack.

"I ... I'd like a panini," I said, desperately pulling my mind together.

"Filling?" she demanded.

I swallowed. "I'd like the brie and red onion chutney."

"Drink?"

"Early grey with a slice of lemon." I stated.

"Right," she said then turned and headed for the kitchen.

I followed her progress, catching sight of the hairs on her chin as she leant through the open door and handed the chef the order. Bright November sunlight, sharp and clear, fell on her face as she reached the counter and the hairs glistened.

My heart thumped a little harder and I scanned the women in the café. There were several who had been at the Women's Institute the night before and from their glances across the room, they were thriving on the gossip. One made a tentative smile until her companion placed a hand over hers and whispered across the table. Both women took a final look then turned to the window, pretending to be interested in the scene outside. One arched her neck to look down the road and I wondered who Hrok was talking to now.

I continued my surveillance of the women, furtively watching as they moved, scanning their faces for any sign of unsightly growth beneath their chins. It was difficult to determine from my position in the room, but there were a couple of contenders for hairy whiskers. Both, I realised, with dread sinking in my belly, had attended the demonstration.

What if it was the cream that was causing rapid growth of unsightly hairs?

They could just be menopausal.

Sure, but the menopause doesn't cause hair growth like that.

Oh, come on! You've seen some of the old women. The hair beneath their chin is as thick and bristly as any man's.

Once they reach a certain age, perhaps, but these women are young. Some aren't even going through the change. You just don't grow beards overnight!

Unless you've applied some malfunctioning magical cream.

Has Aunt Thomasin made a mistake?

Is the cream hexed?

My mind churned the problem over, but it seemed conclusive to me. The only women with unsightly facial hair – that hadn't had it before – were the ones who had been at the Women's Institute on the night I demonstrated the wondrous cream!

The pot of tea was brought to my table, and I poured out a cup with a shaking hand then ate the panini without thought. After I'd finished, I approached the counter to pay. The hair on the waitress' chin looked a little thicker. They curled and had a copper hue, and the sides of her cheeks also had a coppery sheen.

I passed her a twenty-pound note, took my change, thanked her for the meal, and left.

Hrok was hovering close to the village hall. I decided against approaching him and crossed the road and walked back to the shop but, as I pushed the key into the lock, I had a realisation. I hadn't ignored Hrok because I needed to open the shop, or because I wanted to talk to him later, or because I didn't want to talk to him at that moment. I had avoided him because I didn't want to be stigmatised by being associated with him. Shame enveloped me. We were the same. We came from the same people, yet here I was denying him because of the poor opinion of a few spiteful villagers being influenced by a weird cult.

"Shame on you, Livitha Erickson," I said, and withdrew the key from the lock.

I reached Hrok as his conversation with another housewife ended. The woman walked away with a broad smile.

"Hi," I said, squinting against the sun as I looked up to Hrok. I had forgotten how tall he was, and how handsome. I felt none of the arousal of interest that had grabbed me when we first met. Hrok was attractive, certainly, but without the draw of his sorcerer's magick, he wasn't my type.

"Ah, Livitha! How wonderful to see you." He bent forward then kissed the air on either side of my cheeks. "How are you keeping? Busy in the shop? Looking forward to the Night of Good Fires?" He said this with a wry smile and arch of his brow.

"You know about it then?" I asked.

He nodded. "Yes! Another horrible aspect of this village that those troublesome crones omitted to tell me before I became embroiled with them."

I glanced up and down the street. I wanted to talk to Hrok, but in private. "Would you like a cup of tea?" I asked.

He glanced towards the village hall's entrance. "Actually, yes, I would."

We returned to the shop and Hrok waited in the main area whilst I filled the kettle. He was listening to the grandfather clock when I returned with a cup of tea for us both, sans elixir.

"Do you have mice, Liv?" he asked with a confused frown. "Or birds. I'm sure I heard fluttering."

He reached for the key.

"No! Don't open it," I said.

"Oh? Why's that then?"

"Fairies!" I whispered.

He grimaced and pulled his hand away from the key then mouthed 'in there?' whilst pointing at the clock.

I nodded. "They like to be helpful, but they're not keen on visitors."

"Oh, I can handle fairies," he said. "Although they can be a nuisance."

"Tell me about it!" I said, remembering the time they had sent a hideous video of me to my ex as I snored and snorted in sleep.

From inside the grandfather clock came irritated chittering and the buzz of wings.

I held a finger to my lips. "They're very helpful in the shop," I said in a raised voice. "I wouldn't be without them these days."

The chittering subdued and was replaced by a cat-like purring buzz.

"Of course," Hrok said, playing along. "I think they're wonderful creatures."

The purring buzz grew louder.

"And so beautiful!"

I held back a laugh and passed Hrok a mug of tea. He took a sip. "So, Livitha, how are things with you?" He raised his eyebrows and gestured to my eye. "It looks as though life has been exciting for you. Hmm?"

I thought back to the morning and Keira's straggling goat-like beard and then the night at the W.I. and being dragged around the room by my childhood bully.

"Oh, this?" I said touching my cheek. "Just a misunderstanding."

"A misunderstanding?" His brow furrowed. "Is it a ... domestic one?"

He meant Garrett. "Oh! Oh, no. Of course it's not. No, this was from the Women's Institute."

He raised a single brow in surprise. "I've heard they can be a little frosty," he said, "but violent?"

"I said something that upset one of the women. She used to bully me at school."

"She hasn't changed very much then."

I shook my head. "Not at all."

He sighed. "There are some unpleasant people in this village, Livitha. I'm considering leaving."

I didn't like the thought of the villagers being the reason Hrok would leave.

He shivered despite the warmth from the log burner. "There's something in the air. I don't know what, but something ... has changed. The villagers seem antagonistic against us."

"Has something happened?"

He nodded. "Yes. In the past weeks, when the sisters have taken walks, they have been rudely abused. One woman spat at them."

I remembered the woman who had spat at me as a teenager. "There are some who fear us."

"There is nothing to fear. We have done nothing to interfere with their lives."

"I know, but sometimes just being different is enough to inspire hate."

"Which is why we move so frequently—before they have a chance to realise just how different we are." He took another sip of tea. "But the Haligern crones—they have not moved in recent centuries. How so?"

"They've always helped the villagers," I suggested.

He nodded. "They do give off an aura of calm and kindness," he said.

I took a sip of tea. "So, aren't you going to ask me the time?"

He frowned, glanced at the grandfather clock. "Can you not read the clock?"

"Yes, but I've noticed you outside talking to women. You seemed to be asking them the time."

"I was."

"For?"

He sighed. "I thought that if they realised I was a gentleman, someone polite, they may feel a little less inclined to disparage us. My poor girls are upset and I'm getting it in the neck!" He gave another deep and martyred sigh.

"Ah, I see," I said. "And you thought that asking the time was a way to start a conversation with them."

He nodded. "It was a foolish idea. The men don't seem to appreciate it."

"So I saw," I said, remembering the man who had slammed into the lamppost. "Did you use magic on him?"

He nodded. "He was rude and threatening. I taught him a lesson."

"And the woman?"

"Oh, she tripped of her own accord. Nothing to do with me. I did help her up, of course."

Hrok finished his tea, invited me to visit 'any time' then left the shop. I mulled over the situation. Hrok had mentioned that the villagers seemed surly towards them, but he hadn't mentioned the petition that Priscilla was raising against him. There were dark times ahead; I could feel it in my bones.

Chapter Thirteen

As the Night of Good Fires drew near, the energy within Haligern Cottage grew ever more fractious. My aunts quibbled over the slightest thing and seemed to have lost their usual ability to take things in their stride. Mirth and laughter had deserted my home and I was glad that I had to work. Several days after speaking to Hrok, I arrived at the shop with an hour to spare before opening time and busied myself dusting, checking stock levels, and noting down any orders that had been placed via the website. Orders had increased over the past weeks, and I put that down to the time of year. The 'normies' would be celebrating Christmas, whilst we would be celebrating Yule. There was even an order from the Pendlewick crones and another from Effie, the apprentice Vardlokkur, at the Council of Witches. I remembered our meeting, recognising a kindred spirit, and looked forward to meeting her again during the festivities.

With most of the orders packaged, I flipped the sign to 'Open' then disappeared to the back room to make myself another cup of tea. The log burner was throwing out a good amount of heat and the room had grown warm. Glenda's suggestion that we have a sofa in this part of the room was tempting and I imagined a large one in purple velvet. Customers would be able to relax whilst we talked, and I suggested different remedies for their ailments. As the months had passed, my knowledge of my aunts' products had increased, and I was becoming more confident in suggesting solutions for customers' problems and I toyed with the idea of offering consultations. But the problem that bothered me this morning, and which defied a solution, was the contagion of hairy growth among the village housewives.

As customers arrived and browsed our products, I took the opportunity of checking them out, looking for the tell-tale evidence of facial hair. The first three customers had smooth skin without any evidence of wispy growth. However, the fourth, a long-time customer, had sprouted a copper moustache. There was also evidence of curling sideburns. Her appearance confirmed it for me; Aunt Thomasin's cream was the culprit! The first three customers had not been at the demonstration, but the fourth, Mandy Braithwaite, had. At the demonstration she had been fascinated by the transformation of Glenda's skin and had been one of the first to buy a jar of cream. I felt little sympathy though. Mandy had always been Priscilla's faithful, and often unpleasant, sidekick.

She hovered, browsing the shelves until the shop was empty, then walked straight to the counter. Her eyes were hard as they stared into mine.

"Is everything alright, Mandy?" I asked.

"No! Look at my face!" she demanded. "Look what your cream did to me!" She pulled down the headscarf to reveal dark stubble across her chin. The moustache, which had been short and stubby when she entered the shop, now overhung her lips.

"I-"

"You have turned me into a freak!" she spat.

Despite my near conviction that the cream was to fault, I didn't want to admit liability. "Our cream was tested. I use it myself." Both statements were true but felt cowardly. However, until I'd had time to speak to my aunts, I was unsure of how to respond. Admittance of guilt would be an admission of liability and the women could sue, or worse.

She stared at me, then scanned my face. Her shoulders sagged, and her eyes filled with tears. "Then what is causing this? I noticed that some of the other members have hair too. Priscilla is beside herself."

"Priscilla has a hairy chin?" I asked, barely able to keep the smile from my face.

Mandy nodded. "She called me this morning. I know that she can be a ... bitch, and that you're probably happy about it, but she was very brave and made a video call. The growth on her chin makes my beard look like bum fluff," she said with a sigh. "Here, let me show you. I screenshotted it."

The screen was held before me. I snorted, unable to keep the hysteria down. Priscilla Dedman had grown a large and drab-brown curling beard streaked with grey.

"I've told her to shave it off."

I glanced at Mandy. The stubble seemed to be longer. Whatever magick Aunt Thomasin had imbued the cream with, was out of control.

"We're protesting this afternoon, but how can we go out looking like this?" She stabbed a fuchsia nail at her growing coppery beard.

"Well," I said as mischievous thoughts twittered, "you could put on a brave face and own it. Your beard is a lovely shade of copper."

She caught my gaze with a questioning frown.

"It is?"

I nodded, "But I do have some cream that might help," I said and fetched two pots of the growth inhibiting cream. "It works better after you've epilated."

Her glance held a touch of horror. "Epilate? But that's so painful!"

I shrugged my shoulders, relishing this moment of mischief. "It is more effective after epilation."

"Can't we just shave it?"

"Oh, yes, of course you can, but you really need to rip out those hairs for best results."

Her face drained of colour and an image of Priscilla epilating her face flashed in my mind. "That will be seventeen pounds, please."

A frisson of guilt passed over me as she took her bags and left the shop. I had lied, but such was my animosity towards Priscilla that I wanted to cause her pain. She had humiliated me. Dragged me around the schoolroom, watched by a multitude of gloating faces, then punched and kicked me as though it were a particularly vicious playground fight. I touched the side of my face. The flesh felt soft, swollen, and tender. "She deserves it," I said although I lacked real conviction.

Yes, she should be punished for what she did, but what had Mandy done?

She had watched.

Exactly! She had watched.

But she did nothing.

That's not true. She did do something. She chanted and gloated, and who knows, maybe it was her who put in the boot; she was always Priscilla's devoted sidekick at school.

I made another cup of tea, laced it with a drop of elixir, then waited for the next customer. As I waited, I began to think of Garrett's mother. She had the power to ruin my life and I held her in mind with deepening dread. Garrett barely ever spoke of her so I knew little of her character or even what she looked like. I imagined a female version of Garrett but without the broad shoulders. Uncle Tobias had mentioned a painting sent to Garrett's father before they married that was a fair likeness but I had yet to see it. I ruminated on the reasons why she would object to our marriage. I could think of numerous. Would she think my family too low class to be joined to hers? Perhaps she had her eye on another family to help create bonds with through marriage. Or maybe she wanted grandchildren. My heart sank. I was too old, I felt sure, to give Garrett a child and my barren years with Pascal, despite the numerous efforts to become pregnant, were a clear sign I was infertile.

But Garrett loves you!

Does that matter? If his mother has the final say on whether we can marry or not, then there's an end to it.

Live together then. You don't need to marry.

But I want to marry him.

Elope! Run away!

The doorbell above the shop's door tinkled and another customer entered. I turned my attention to them, thankful for the interruption of my painful thoughts. As the hours wore on, I became tired. The incident at the WI had made me angry, but the anger was brittle and sharp, and wearing. I began to flag and, during a lull after serving several customers, I decided to close the shop. Mandy had mentioned a protest but caught up in the sight of hair growing like weeds on her face, I hadn't thought to ask what it was about. However, if Priscilla was involved it was likely to do with the petition to have Hrok's house of ill-repute shut down. As the clock struck two, I locked the door and made my way to the centre of the village.

Chapter Fourteen

The noise caught my attention first and as I stepped into the village square, I was surprised at the number of people gathered there. Behind them a new wooden post, at least eight feet tall, protruded from the grassed area where the yearly burning of Hetty Yikkar's effigy would take place. Branches and logs were already piled around its base. The sight hit me like a punch and dark clouds shifting in from the moors added to the sense of foreboding.

Apart from a few bemused onlookers, most of the women held placards or banners. Some appeared to be handmade whilst others were professionally produced. 'Purity is Joy!' was printed on several, along with 'Keep our village pure.' Several of the handmade ones had a red circle with a diagonal red line struck through 'Haligern Whores'. Others had 'Shut the Whorehouse Down'.

Across the square, hanging back in the lane that filtered from the direction of Leodrune House, I noticed Hrok. As I watched him watching the crowd, he stepped out of the light and blended into the shadows becoming invisible. It was a practiced and sleek manoeuvre. I was impressed and made a mental note to ask him how he had achieved it with the hope he would teach me the skill.

Priscilla stood before the post and, for one moment, the image of her roped to the stake with branches burning at her feet, grew vivid in my mind.

Unkind, Liv! She is a horror, but being burned alive is a touch too much justice.

The thought of her being punished was intensely satisfying and I became determined that she would suffer, in some way, for her bullying and the attack at the W.I.

Becoming a hairy monster isn't enough?

No. I didn't do that to her, someone else did.

So, you think the hairiness could be a form of punishment?

I pondered upon these thoughts. Yes, the plague of hairiness among the village housewives could be a form of punishment. But by whom? And why? What had the women done to deserve it?

As I continued to explore these ideas, Priscilla began to speak, and I focused on her instead. I moved through the crowd for a better view. Priscilla's beard, dark brown and peppered with grey, was missing, but a closer inspection revealed why. Priscilla had run with the advice I gave Mandy and epilated her beard! Her chin was a shade of the rawest red although her top lip had already begun to darken with new growth. Laughter bubbled and I snorted whilst trying to keep it inside. It was uncharitable of me to find enjoyment in her pain, but I was raw from the experience of being beaten and humiliated in the school room. Just behind her stood Mandy, surprisingly un-epilated and with her beard in full view. Its coppery hue glinted in the sunlight that found a path through the darkening clouds.

I slipped between the women to stand at the front of the protestors. Priscilla held a microphone to her mouth. A high-pitch squeal split the air. She flinched and frowned at Mandy who responded by bending down and fiddling with the amplifier. The noise adjusted and Priscilla began to speak. What followed was pure fearmongering vitriol aimed at Hrok and the Slawston sisters. It was greeted by shouts of agreement from the crowd. After she had finished her diatribe, Prudence Wellwisher took her place to a round of applause from the protestors. She held up a hand in thanks and the crowd grew silent.

"Remember, ladies," she began, "the Carmichael prostitutes are very beautiful. They have long limbs and slender thighs, pert breasts, and voluptuous curves. They are just the kind of women that your husbands want to bed!"

The gathered women chuntered.

"Think, ladies! Your husbands come back to *you* after a hard day's work. A woman who has borne children and shows the scars of that birthing in her flabby and stretch-marked belly. A woman who has become thankful for the forgiveness of stretchy jeggings and the cellulite they hide. A woman who places no value in making herself appealing to her man. A woman who, tired after a day of childcare, cooking, and cleaning, often turns down his advances and denies him his conjugal rights! *You* no longer satisfy your husbands' desires!"

The crowd remained silent.

"But do you know who will?" She paused for effect. "The women in that house of ill-repute." She stabbed a finger in the direction of Leodfrune house. "The sexy and subservient women in that house will gladly satisfy his every desire. Do you want your husbands to become perverts? Only aroused by beautiful women?"

"No!" the crowd shouted.

"Then we must rid the village of these women! You must save your husbands from their grasping hands."

"They can have mine," a woman beside me muttered. I noticed she didn't carry a placard. "I'll swap him for Roger."

Behind me I heard a snort of laughter. "Looking at them, I'd say their husbands' would be glad to be stolen".

Hrok!

I turned to him. The space was empty, although I sensed his energy. An invisible hand tugged mine.

"Come over here, Livitha," Hrok's voice whispered in my ear.

Unseen fingers grasped my hand and without comment, I allowed Hrok to guide me to the edge of the protest and then up a quiet lane.

Hrok materialised as the shimmering façade of magical energy that surrounded him thinned then disappeared. He lacked his usual smile.

"I'm so sorry about this," I said.

"It's not your fault. I put the blame squarely on the shoulder of those troublesome crones!"

"They weren't to know-"

"Apart from the witch that was burned here in this very square!" He shook his head. "Those crones lied to me, Livitha. There is a strong and vicious puritanical streak in this village that goes back centuries. They lied to me!"

"The villagers are being influenced by a new cult," I explained. "A woman called Prudence Wellwisher-"

He snorted. "That's not a real name!"

"I thought that too. Anyway, she's a newcomer and set up this weird cult that promotes purity or something. They meet in the village hall. It's very popular among the housewives."

"Hah! Things never change but it is the Slawston crones I am angry with. They said there had never been trouble for our kind here, but now I know different. Granted, I would celebrate the burning of Hetty Yikkar too, but ..." He gave a deep and disgruntled sigh. "This is not a village I can live in."

"Are you going to leave?"

"I have no choice."

"Where will you go?"

"I've been scouting around. There's another realm I could move to."

Another realm, not just another country. I was fascinated. "Ooh! Tell me about this other realm."

He glanced towards the crowd who were now listening to Priscilla speak. "Well, it's much like this one was hundreds of years ago—sparsely populated and the inhabitants are true to their pagan roots, not like this place. I'm afraid the ideologies that took hold here have twisted people's minds. They're so ... so bloodthirsty! And the word is that there are forces about that have put in place a cull and control operation. History is cyclical my dear and this place is about due for another visit from the four horsemen."

"The four horsemen are biblical," I said, a little confused. "We're pagans."

"Ah, yes, but they are used to describe a universal phenomenon."

"War, famine, pestilence, and death."

"Yes, beware the rider on a pale horse!"

"Or giants."

"Yes, giants too. Horrid creatures and they make such a terrible mess. It will be such a refreshing change to live a simpler life. All this white, crystal, and glamour, is such a drain. I'm forever having to wipe away smudges and shampoo the upholstery! But the girls wanted to be 'modern.'" He gave a martyred sigh.

He had talked about moving in the singular. Was he going to leave the Slawston sisters behind? I was about to ask him if he intended to take the Slawston crones with him when Priscilla's voice cut through the air, and he flinched.

"Onward, ladies!" her voice boomed through a loud hailer and the crowd turned towards us.

Hrok stepped behind me then disappeared.

The protestors surged forward, banners held high, and I decided to walk with them. I had never been to a protest before and was curious how it would end. I'd seen them on television, of course, and they were portrayed as either being ill-attended or violent occasions where police vans were set on fire with riot police out in force. The village effort amounted to about thirty men and women, some with buggies, moving at a slow pace. At the front, Priscilla continued to blare instructions through her loud hailer.

"Where are we going?" I asked a young mother walking beside me.

"We're stopping outside the brothel and then Kevin Parker's house."

"Why Kevin Parker's house?" I asked.

"He's a parish councillor and his wife works in the housing department at the Council. We want him to put pressure on her to get the Carmichael's evicted. They rent, so it's easier. The landlord can be forced to evict them."

"Priscilla is going all out to get them kicked out of the village then," I said.

"She is. She's a force to be reckoned with when she wants to be."

Among other things! I couldn't disagree and continued to walk beside the woman. As the mob reached Leodfrune House and Priscilla once again raised the loud hailer to her mouth, I had no stomach to listen and decided to return to the shop.

"Burn the witch!" The words were distorted as squealing notes split the air.

I halted and turned. Priscilla had found something to stand on and was head and shoulders above the crowd. She was scowling and stabbed a finger in my direction. "Burn the witch!" she screamed, her demented voice carrying over the crowd as they turned to stare. "Burn the witch!"

Chapter Fifteen

Talking to Hrok, and then listening to the spitefulness of the women's chanting, had taken its toll, and I returned to the shop with an oppressive sense of foreboding. Aunt Beatrice had said she felt the oncoming trouble in her bones, and I was beginning to believe that she was right. The Night of Good Fires was only days away and the village was in uproar about a sorcerer and his concubines and was blaming Haligern Coven for an affliction of hairiness. I had no stomach to face any more customers and so locked the shop and drove back home.

"Whatever is the matter?" Aunt Thomasin asked as I entered the house. She wafted the air in front of her and took a step backwards towards the kitchen. "You're bringing some very damp energy inside. Beatrice!" she called as she stepped through the doorway. "Lay some more logs on the fire, Livitha is very damp!"

I gave a martyred sigh and made my way into the kitchen. Renweard raised his head, whined then turned away from me. Benny squawked from the curtain pole, and Bess trotted across to the wolf hound, curling up on his belly as though for protection. She shivered then shuffled closer.

"Dear me! I see what you mean," said Aunt Beatrice and immediately walked to the hearth and threw several logs into the fire. Sparks flew and Bess yelped as embers floated above her.

"What has happened?" asked Aunt Thomasin.

"Sit down, child," said Aunt Beatrice. "I have tea in the pot and crumble in the oven."

I shook my head. "I'm fine," I lied.

"Crumble?" asked Aunt Beatrice.

I shook my head. My aunts exchanged concerned glances as I slumped down in the chair beside the fire. Sparks crackled and the tips of my fingers fizzed.

"Look at her aura," said Aunt Thomasin. "It is almost black."

"Poor child," said Aunt Beatrice as she poured tea into my favourite cup. "And to refuse crumble, even when I have offered it before our meal."

"Unheard of," said Aunt Thomasin.

Aunt Beatrice handed me the cup. Coiling steam rose towards the ceiling. I accepted the drink then sank a little further into myself, enjoying the morose sensation. The entire village was against us. They hated us.

"Tsk!" Aunt Beatrice's lips thinned.

"What is it?" asked Aunt Thomasin.

"She believes that the village has taken against us."

"They're out for our blood!" I blurted. "And they want Hrok and the Slawston crones run out of the village."

My memories returned to the village square and the chanting. One woman had screamed about witches. Another had called for us to be burned at the stake.

Aunt Beatrice shivered. "I knew it! I knew that Hetty would bring us down one day."

"Whatever are you talking about, sister?" asked Loveday as she entered the room. She stopped mid-stride, wafting at the air. "Whatever has happened. The air is so muggy."

"Livitha has filled it with damp energy," Aunt Thomasin explained.

"Livitha!" Aunt Loveday moved across the room with speed. "Why ... I have never seen you in such a state. It must stop." She turned to my aunts. "This is pure self-pity."

"I cannot say that I blame her," said Aunt Beatrice coming to my defence. "The poor child was set upon by a woman who bullied her at school and today she has had another bad experience. She claims that the village has turned against us."

"I have heard rumours," said Loveday. "Mrs. Greatwell mentioned that a protest had been organised against the Slawston coven."

"They want to burn witches," I said through my stupor.

"Do they know that the Slawston sisters are witches?"

Aunt Loveday shook her head. "No. We can be thankful for that. What they are protesting against is their unconventional living arrangements."

"It was foolish to set up a harem in a small village," said Aunt Thomasin. "He could have got away with it in a larger place."

"They objected to that at first," Loveday continued, "but they have now come to believe that the sisters are prostitutes and that Hrok is running a brothel."

"They think they'll steal their husbands," I said.

"Hah! Given what hairy brutes they have become, I should think the men would quite gladly run away."

"That's what Hrok said."

"When did you see Hrok?"

"This afternoon at the protest. We both left when they started chanting 'burn the witches.'

"Hsst!"

"And so close to the Night!"

I took a sip of tea, the wet blanket of stupor it pulled over me soothing my fraught senses.

"The Slawston sisters must leave," said Aunt Thomasin. "Before a new witch hunt begins."

I shook my head. "It's not them they want to burn," I said.

"Then who?" Aunt Loveday asked.

"Us!" I said, unable to keep the emotion from my voice. "It is us they want to burn!"

"I told you!" said Aunt Beatrice her voice high with tension. "I told you that Hetty would have her revenge one day!".

"Hush, Beatrice!" scolded Loveday. "The woman is dead and not about to wreak revenge on anyone in this room."

"But she could-"

"Now stop it, Beatrice, you are causing worry for the child."

"We should leave this village!" Aunt Beatrice continued. "We should leave until they have forgotten about us!".

The room grew silent, and I listened through a fog of self-pity, fear, and elixir-induced stupor to Aunt Beatrice's fretful suggestions about moving away from Haligern.

"What if the grimoires have been found and someone is using them against us?"

The air crackled and sparks shot to the beams above Aunt Loveday. "Now, Beatrice, your anxiety is getting out of hand. You must cease and desist with this nonsense."

"But the books are still lost-"

Aunt Loveday raised a silencing hand. "Now is not the time, Beatrice."

"But she could have a point, Loveday," said Aunt Thomasin.

Loveday's aura shimmered and where it shone an iridescent purple it grew black. "If I hear one more word about those ... those poisonous books I will explode!" A shower of sparks erupted and she turned with a swing of her long skirts and swept out of the kitchen.

"Why is she so upset about some lost books?" I asked.

"Oh, it's nothing, dear," Aunt Euphemia said. "Warm yourself by the fire and have another cup of tea. It's nothing to worry about, nothing at all."

I was not convinced by her words but, sodden with fatigue, I remained by the fire and eventually ate a bowl of crumble with an extra helping of custard then took myself to bed. I had a difficult night filled with dreams of witches being captured and tied to posts. There were no fires in the dreams, but the stench of smoke was so intense it seemed real.

Chapter Sixteen

I woke to the rumble of deep voices, the stench of smoke, and a pressure on my belly.

"You're awake. Finally!"

"Pork ... later," I mumbled.

"Yes, that would be nice, but beforehand, I suggest you wake before the house is burned to the ground."

"What?"

"It's a freakshow, Livitha!" Lucifer declared spiking my duvet with his claws as he pawed it. "And the husbands are rioting!"

My stomach did a watery flip as the call of an angry voice sank into my consciousness. "Rioting?"

"Yes, I'm afraid it's pitchforks at dawn—again. Look out of the window."

With another call of "Burn the witches!" reaching my ears, I threw the duvet aside and padded over to the window, oblivious to the chill in the room.

I peered through the glass. A group of villagers had gathered. Pitchforks had been replaced with placards, although one held a burning torch to light the dark morning.

I let the curtain fall back.

"Don't just stand there," demanded Lucifer. "Do something!"

"Like what?"

"Use your magic against them."

"And prove that we are the witches they accuse us of being?"

"You are the witches they accuse you of being."

"No, we're not."

"Yes, you are."

"We're not, Lucifer. We're not bad witches."

"But you've turned their wives into hairy beasts with your magic," he quipped. "The Women's Institute looks as though it is part of the Talbot clan," Lucifer snorted. "They'll be teaching beard care instead of jam making next." With this his shoulders heaved.

"It wasn't on purpose. Aunt Thomasin's magick went awry, that's all."

"Aunt Thomasin's magick never goes awry. If the women are growing hair because of her magick then she meant for them to grow hair."

"I don't believe that. The cream was meant to help their skin look younger."

"But they grew hair instead."

"Yes, which means Aunt Thomasin's cream went wrong somewhere along the production line."

"In all my considerable years of knowing your aunts, I have never once come across a spell of theirs that went wrong. You on the other hand ..."

I turned to the malicious feline. "What exactly are you saying?"

"I'm saying," he said, "that if the magick in the cream went awry, then it was your fault. You hexed the women. You are the reason for the Haligern Hotties turning into the Haligern Horror-billies."

"Horror-billies isn't even a word, Lucifer."

"Perhaps not, but the women now have more than a passing resemblance to Billy goats." He snorted and his shoulders heaved. "And anyway, it should be a word. It is an excellent description of the hirsute monstrosities those poor men are having to share their beds with. I would riot if my wife turned into an ugly goat. Come to think of it, horror-billies is also perfect to describe Old Mawde and that hideous curmudgeon Hegelina Fekkit."

A thought crossed my mind. "Do you think this could be Old Mawde's doing?"

He shook his head. "No. Whilst she's cursed – and I have to let you know that since you have reneged on your promise to release her, she is more scathing and filled with ire than ever-"

"I didn't promise to release her."

"You did!"

"Anyway, she threatened to harm us once free, so I couldn't lift the curse. She's just too dangerous."

"Well, be careful when you milk her next. That's all I'm saying."

"Warning heeded," I replied.

"Now, let's get back to the hairy calamity that has befallen the ... ladies of Haligern." He snickered. "I do hope they don't catch the attention of journalists. Can you imagine it? It would go viral – as they say – and the Haligern Horror-billies would be splashed across the newspapers."

"And the television. And social media," I said as another chant of 'burn the witches' began.

"They could call it 'The Real Housewives of Haligern: Horror-billy Special."

"Terrible," I said.

Lucifer sighed. "Anyway, my point is that your Aunt Thomasin is innocent in all of this."

"But-"

"Unless ..."

"Unless?"

"Unless she did it on purpose. She is far too experienced to make such a mistake."

"There is no way she did it on purpose," I said.

"Then there is only one other explanation."

"Which is?"

"That it is your fault. You are the only one with a poor grasp of her magical powers around here."

"I did nothing! I had absolutely nothing to do with making the cream. Plus, I was the guinea pig. See!" I held out my palm and created a small witch light, enough for Lucifer to see my skin but not enough to alert the men outside that I was awake.

"It is smooth. You have been plucking the hairs. So what?"

"No, I have not plucked the hairs. My point is that I have been using the same cream. It had no effect on me."

"So, you hexed it after production. And I know why?"

"Why?"

"Because you are an eternal victim."

"Wha-"

"You are so churned up with hatred towards Priscilla Dedman that you hexed the cream knowing full well of the consequences."

"I did not."

"And now the coven is in jeopardy."

"But I-"

"There is only one answer! You must sacrifice yourself to clear your aunts' names. Allow them to burn you at the stake."

I stood unable to speak, my heart knocking against my chest, breath caught.

"What do you think?" he asked licking his paw. "It is a good solution, I believe."

"You want me to burn at the stake?"

"No. I didn't say that. I just said that, given your obvious guilt, you should fess up and take the consequences. I believe they call it taking one for the team. So, admit your crime and let them burn you at the stake."

"That is ridiculous."

"Is it? Is it really?"

"Yes."

"Hmm," he said, seeming to ponder the issue. "Then I have one more suggestion."

"Which is?"

"That you solve the crime instead of wallowing in self-pity and crying into your milk about a big bad bully!"

"Lucifer! I-" My words stalled.

He tapped his tail against the carpet then sauntered to the door. "Which is it to be, Livitha Erikson, daughter of shame? Are you going to embrace your true self or crumble and let your aunts be burned to a crisp?"

He disappeared through the gap in the door leaving me open mouthed in a vortex of shame and realisation that the cat was right. With the mob chanting 'burn the witch', I made my way downstairs. My aunts were gathered in the kitchen.

"The last time we had a pitchfork mob at the door, it was Hetty's fault.

"Hsst!"

"No, I do believe we had a pitchfork mob only a few months ago."

"That's right, they accused us of causing that sinkhole that devoured the new estate."

"Oh, how I wish I had cast that spell!"

"Well, this time they think we have hexed their wives!"

"And turned them into horror-billies," I said.

All four aunts turned to look at me.

"It's what Lucifer calls the hairy women. Horror-billies – like Billy goats."

"It's true, they do look horrifying. A beard never was a good look for a woman, although I did see one once in a freak show that came to the village but that was ... oh ..."

"1898," said Aunt Euphemia. "I remember it well. If I recall, the circus inspired a pitchfork mob then, too."

"The villagers do get rather testy around newcomers."

"And freaks."

"Which is why they're freaking out about their homegrown freaks," Lucifer snorted then slinked between my ankles. "Is this a bad time to ask for a saucer of port and a bowl of roast-"

"Yes!" Five voices answered him in unison.

I peered through the kitchen curtain. "They're not going away."

"We should speak to them."

"They're bound to be rude."

"Yes, but only one has a weapon."

"This is a déjà vu," said Aunt Beatrice with a quiver in her voice.

"Beatrice ... show a little backbone, please."

Aunts Thomasin and Euphemia peered through the curtain.

"They're in there!" shouted a man.

"They've seen us!"

"Of course they have," said Aunt Loveday "We live here. They know that."

"Then what are we to do?"

"We do not panic."

"I'm going to talk to them," I said.

Four pairs of eyes turned to me. Lucifer snorted.

"Are you sure?" asked Aunt Beatrice.

Waiting for my reaction, the aunts remained silent. I had expected protest.

"I ... yes. I shall go to them and explain that we had nothing to do with their wives becoming hairy."

"But what if we did."

"You did," said Lucifer.

"Pardon, Lucifer?"

"Ignore him," I said. "He has some crackpot idea that Aunt Thomasin did it on purpose or that I did it in error because I'm rubbish at magick."

"You are," he said and raised his head, looking at me with defiant eyes.

"How dare you, Lucifer," said Aunt Thomasin. "I would never hex the creams. It would destroy our business."

"And our reputation."

"And unleash the pitchfork mob!" said Aunt Beatrice with a fearful glance towards the curtains.

"Then my logic is sound. If you did not hex the cream, then Livitha did."

"Lucifer, that is preposterous. I had nothing to do with the production of the cream."

"But you collected the herbs," said Aunt Beatrice.

"Exactly," said Lucifer. "And I suggested that Livitha offer herself as sacrifice for the burning."

Chapter Seventeen

All four eyes turned to Lucifer. Silence fell among my aunts, but the air began to crackle. He made no sign of noticing.

"Unless, of course, Livitha can prove who did it. I am sick of her wallowing in self-pity."

"I was beaten up!" I said in my defence.

"You should have fought back," he retorted. "If you had fought back as a child, Priscilla Dedman would never have dared to bully you."

"He has a point," agreed Aunt Euphemia.

"She bullied me for years!" I complained.

"Exactly!" his voice was a high pitch. "Now, with respect, I suggest that you confront the mob at the door just as you should have confronted Priscilla Dedman in the playground. Send them away with a flea in their ear and then set to work solving the mystery."

The energy in the kitchen remained fractious but the sparking stopped.

"He's right," declared Loveday. "We cannot cower here. If someone hexed the cream - which is the only reasonable explanation - then we must discover just who it was and why they have done it."

"What if he is right, and it was me?"

Aunt Loveday shook her head. "You cannot place a hex on something just by picking herbs, Livitha."

I relaxed a little.

"And if she wanted revenge against Priscilla, I'm sure she wouldn't have made the other ladies suffer too," suggested Aunt Euphemia.

Murmurs of agreement followed.

"So, Livitha, although I hate to admit it, Lucifer is right."

"I should let them burn me at the stake?"

"No, of course not, whyever would we think that?"

"It's what Lucifer suggested I do, as penance!"

Aunt Loveday shook her head and cast Lucifer a hard stare. He hissed and retreated behind my legs. "Lucifer has a particularly unique way of making us realise ways forward," she continued. "Go out there and deal with the men. Reassure them that we were not involved but that we will help their wives. Then send them away!"

"With force, if necessary," added Aunt Beatrice.

"I'm sure it won't be necessary."

With my aunts peering into the hallway from the kitchen doorway, I opened the front door. At least ten men, some hooded, stood outside.

"Finally!" a man towards the back of the group grumbled.

"Cowards!" another spat.

"Good morning," I said holding back the quiver in my voice. My fingers tingled and sparks hit the door. I willed my energies to grow calm, taking a breath to ease the tension.

The crowd grew quiet, all eyes directed onto me. I felt their anger as a wave but alongside it was fear, a dangerous mixture.

One man stepped forward, then back again, his placard held as though it were a pitchfork he wanted to spear me with.

"How can I help you?" I asked.

"You've cast a spell on our women!" a bearded man from the back shouted.

"You're all witches!" a shrill voice shouted. "You've hexed the village with your evil magic!"

I focused on the voice. It came from a hooded man with a large dark beard with a white stripe at its centre. It reminded me of a badger's coat. As I scanned the group there appeared to be women among them although it was difficult to be sure. The early morning light remained grey and although the light above the step cast yellow light around me much of the angry mob was in shadow.

The energy from the group was menacing, and fear could make them spiteful and reckless. I had to face them without sign of weakness. "What you're saying is not true in any way, shape, or form," I declared.

"Then why are our women hairy? It came overnight."

"She cast a spell!" The voice came from the direction of the striped beard, and I began to doubt, despite the bulk, that it was a male and was instead a tall and broad woman.

"The beards grew the day after you sold them your cream at the W.I." a man at the front growled, "and now my wife looks like a man!"

"I'm very sorry that your wives have become hairy, but it has nothing to do with our cream. I use it myself and it has reduced the hairs on my face."

I realised my mistake the moment I uttered the sentence. The crowd surged forward, and several torches pointed into my face. Grumbling spread among them as I squinted against the light.

"She's right, there's no hair on her face."

The light became less intense as the villagers moved back but the hooded figure with the badger-like beard pushed through the crowd to the front.

"She's a liar!" the hooded figure seethed. "That cream was contaminated!"

I realised the broad-shouldered figure was a woman.

"But her face isn't hairy," a man beside her said.

"That's because she's lying. She's a witch. It's what witches do."

This was followed by grumbling among the crowd. I had several choices: a) deny I was a witch b) continue to deny that the cream was contaminated, c) scare the villagers off the property with magick. C was the worst choice and would prove that we were witches. A felt wrong; I was a witch, and I was proud of that fact. B was the only option but would just lead to a continuation of the confrontation unless I offered something more.

"I'm sure that we can settle this. We're happy to have the cream tested at a laboratory. It will prove that there are no contaminants."

"How do we know that you'll do it?"

"I promise that we will."

"Not good enough," a man shouted. "Witches are liars. That is well known."

His statement irked me. It was a malicious lie, and I began to struggle to keep anger from showing in my voice. I took a breath before replying. "My aunts and I have only ever done good for the village of Haligern." This was neither a denial nor acceptance that we were witches. "We make ointments and creams that help your ailments, nothing more."

This seemed to sooth the rabble and it grew quiet. One man at the back turned and began to walk towards the gate.

"No!" the badger-bearded woman shouted. "She's a witch and she has hexed the women of Haligern. She must be burned. The scriptures tell us so! A witch must be burned. It is the only way to stop them."

I realised then that the badger-bearded woman was Priscilla Dedman.

"Actually, the scriptures don't say to burn witches. In Exodus it says, 'Thou shalt not suffer a witch to live' and in Leviticus it says that a wizard should be stoned to death."

"That's good enough for me!" Priscilla shouted. "Stone her!"

The group began to grumble and argue whether stoning or burning was the right way forward.

"We should go home!" the man who had quoted the bible said. "We can settle this like the lady says, by testing the cream."

"They could fake the results. How are we to trust them?"

"Burn the witch!" Priscilla shouted.

"I promise you that it will all be done properly," I shouted above the clamour.

"She will give us a jar of uncontaminated cream!"

"It's hexed! She has poisoned our women!"

A small section of the crowd was becoming agitated, led by Priscilla. My anger flared. She was the one inciting hate against us—again. As I scanned the crowd, I recognised several other women from the village.

I stepped onto the driveway to confront her. Priscilla was a tall woman and, with her full and badger-like beard, a forbidding sight. The villagers grew quiet.

I was back in the playground, once again being tormented by the tallest girl in the class who had taken a deep and abiding dislike against me.

My heart beat hard. My fingers fizzed. The ancient voices began to speak.

But I had to stand up to her without resorting to magick.

"You are full of hate, Priscilla Dedman," I said. "You are a mean and spiteful woman just as you were a mean and spiteful child."

Her eyes narrowed and her top lip pulled to the side as she sneered. "And what does that make you?" she spat. "Look at my face! She pulled down her hood. The men around her groaned, repulsed. Her eyebrows had grown long and overarching. The side of her face sported mutton chop sideburns that ended in a spectacularly curling beard and a moustache that could be plaited. Hair even protruded from her nostrils and ears.

"You've made my wife hideous!" a man beside her said. "And she wasn't a looker to start with!"

Priscilla turned her scornful eyes to him. He cowered and took a step away from his hairy bride.

"Burn the witch!" the husband shouted.

"Grab her!" Priscilla screeched.

Maniacal hatred shone in her eyes as she launched herself towards me. My reaction was instinctive. Without thought I raised my hands to fend her off and began reciting ancient words.

Taller than me by almost a foot, Priscilla grabbed my hair. Follicles still sore from her last attack became raw. "I'll kill you!" I screamed, enraged.

She dragged me to the ground. Memories of the playground and the schoolroom merged. The noise from the surrounding mob was chaotic.

Not this time!

The grip on my hair released.

A woman screamed.

Priscilla staggered.

I stood upright and took a step towards the house.

Priscilla stood to her full height, but her face was contorted, the scowl replaced by confusion as the magick began its work. Bones began to warp, and hair parted as bony protrusions appeared at the top of her head. The crowd gasped and began to chunter.

What have I done?

You've turned her into a goat, Liv. And they all saw you do it!

The crowd grew silent.

Priscilla began to jerk, her body in spasm as it changed, the horns growing from her skull more pronounced. Her fingers melded together as her nose widened and lengthened. Her teeth became tombstone-like. The pupils distorted, becoming a horizontal lozenge.

Priscilla's husband screamed.

The crowd backed away.

As Priscilla's horns grew, they curled.

"She's the devil!" screamed a black-bearded woman.

Unsure whether they were talking about me or Priscilla, I held up my hand. Sparks flew from the tips of my fingers.

"Go home!" The command came from a voice hoarse with shouting, deep and guttural. "Leave Haligern land! Now!"

The remaining villagers turned and fled as my hated bully dropped to her knees whilst her hands and feet morphed into hooves.

"Well," said Lucifer as the last villager disappeared through the gate and Priscilla bleated whilst running in tight, and frantic, circles, udder swinging, "that went well!"

Chapter Eighteen

After reeling with shock, I gathered my senses, grabbed Priscilla's horns and walked to the field where I left her in the care of Old Mawde and Hegelina Fekkit. After explaining exactly why the witch-hating woman had become a goat, I returned to the kitchen. The energy was fractious, and my aunts were bickering among themselves. Sparks hit the beams. Benny cawed from the curtain pole whilst Renweard and Bess pretended to be asleep by the fire.

All four turned their attention to me as I walked into the room. The air crackled.

"I've put her in the field," I said.

They remained silent. The air was thick with disapproval.

"I ... it just happened! I didn't think-"

Aunt Loveday held up a silencing hand. "It will teach the woman a lesson, in the meantime, we must discover who has hexed the village women. Only the strongest of hexes could have caused such hairy monstrosities. Whilst we're doing that, we will have to think very carefully about how to deal with the villagers."

"We should take a vacation from Haligern," stated Aunt Thomasin.

Aunt Beatrice nodded. "It is time. I feel it in my bones."

"A vacation?"

"Time away to allow the gossip to subside and lose itself in memory."

"But that will take years," I stated. "Decades!"

"They still celebrate Hetty's burning."

"Centuries!"

"And we do not want to join Hetty as part of their celebrations," said Aunt Euphemia. "I think Loveday is right. It may be time to move elsewhere for a while."

"How long for?"

"Several generations should do it. Until we are no longer part of living memory."

"Eighty years," suggested Aunt Beatrice.

"Ninety to be safe."

Murmurs of agreement passed among my aunts.

"You can't!" I stated. The implications of what they were suggesting were profound. We couldn't leave Haligern!

"It's what we witches do, when our presence becomes problematic, Livitha, and those men and women just watched you transmogrify one of their leaders into a goat. There can be no doubt now that we are indeed the witches they accuse us of being."

"We're not the witches they accuse us of being. We're good! We only help."

"And turn them into goats," said Aunt Loveday. "Anyway, enough of this. Our priority must be to discover who has hexed the cream."

"Although I agree that the women must be hexed," said Aunt Thomasin, "I do not for one second believe that my cream is at fault."

Aunts Beatrice and Euphemia exchanged doubting looks.

"I second Livitha's earlier suggestion," said Aunt Loveday. "We should test the cream for any sign of contaminant or ... overuse of magic."

"Overuse of magic!" blurted Aunt Euphemia. "Those women have been hexed!"

"So, what is it exactly that you are suggesting, Loveday?" Aunt Thomasin said, hands placed firmly on her slender hips. "What exactly are you accusing me of?" Her pale skin had become flushed and there were flashes of anger in her eyes.

"Oh, Thomasin," said Aunt Beatrice in a voice that sounded synthetically soothing, "I'm sure that Loveday is not accusing you of anything."

"Quite the contrary, Beatrice, it sounds to me as though she is accusing me of being a black witch or working with one of Hetty Yikkar's spells!"

Loveday's eyes shot wide open, and she clamped her gaze on Aunt Thomasin with more than a passing flicker of anger on her face. It grew dark and then her eyes narrowed. I had never seen my aunt's mood switch so quickly and sensed the power of her magic like a pressure against my body. It was oppressive and I stepped towards the door as sparks began to crackle.

"What do you know of Hetty Yikkar's spell books?" she asked with a flash of venom.

All eyes were on Thomasin who suddenly seemed deflated. "Nothing!" she said.

Aunt Loveday took a step closer.

"Oh, dear," sighed Aunt Beatrice. "Hetty's at it again."

"I thought she burned at the stake in 1487," I said still fascinated at the scene unfolding before me.

"Oh, she did, but her evil lives on. She's a trigger point for your aunt. What's the modern word, some convoluted thing about nerves being shot."

"Shellshock?" suggested Aunt Euphemia.

"PTSD?" I offered.

"One of them," Aunt Beatrice said. "Whatever it is, Loveday suffers from it. She riles like a tiger when anyone mentions Hetty's books."

"The lost grimoires? But they're lost."

"They are," said Loveday, "but still incredibly dangerous to those who discover them, which is why I would like to know why Thomasin mentioned having knowledge of them."

All eyes turned to Aunt Thomasin.

"I know nothing of them," she said in earnest.

"Then why did you accuse Loveday of accusing you of using them in your anti-ageing potion? A potion that has shown itself to be spectacularly effective."

Thomasin smiled. "Thank you, Euphemia. It was."

"Until it wasn't," said Aunt Loveday, her face dour. "And then it became a blight on the faces of the housewives."

"It's how Hetty would have used magick," said Aunt Euphemia. "She would draw them in with flattery and promises and then, boom! Hit them where it hurts."

"She was a devil."

"She was certainly evil, sister. I must agree with that."

"There is no evidence that my cream is the cause of the outbreak of hairiness among the housewives."

"We agreed to test it," I said, "to confirm if the cream was at fault."

"Livitha is right," said Aunt Euphemia. "I think we're all getting rather worked up over nothing."

"And going round in circles."

"The housewives of Haligern suffering a bout of hairiness-"

"They're not just hairy," quipped Lucifer, "they are fur covered monsters! They put the Talbot shifters to shame. The Talbots are quite offended apparently as they believe that the hairy housewives are making fun of them. And with their sire having fled the village to avoid arrest, their honey badger temperaments are being stirred to retaliation. I dread the full moon, I really do."

"Oh, dear. Thomasin, what have you done?"

"It wasn't me!"

"So, you don't have one of Hetty Yikkar's lost books?" prodded Aunt Loveday.

"Of course I don't."

A memory suddenly rose in my mind. "I think ..." The picture became clear. "I think that the housewives began to become hairy *before* I gave the demonstration at the WI. In fact, it was before we had even sold a tub of the cream."

"Oh?"

"Yes. And it was Priscilla! We were in the café and she came in with her clipboard. I noticed then that she had dark and curling whiskers beneath her chin and some on her top lip!"

"Some women do suffer-"

"Yes, but everything else about her was immaculate. Her hair was perfectly groomed, her make up just right, but there were hairs beneath her chin, and they were *curling*! No woman so well-groomed would leave curly hairs on her jowl!"

"She has a point."

"And! And there was another woman. I remember her clearly now. I had seen her the previous day in the café – they do a wonderful jam sponge and custard on a Monday."

"No wonder you're only having one helping of crumble, Livitha," Aunt Beatrice tutted.

"And not losing any weight because of it."

I ignored the jibe about my overly generous middle. "Anyway, on the previous day, she was completely hair free, but in the shop, she had quite a crop."

Aunt Beatrice sniggered. "In the shop she had quite a crop!"

Aunt Loveday tutted. "Yes, thank you, Beatrice. Proceed with your evidence, Livitha."

"Are we in a court of law now," Aunt Thomasin said with a hint of derision.

Aunt Loveday's lips pursed momentarily.

"And," I exclaimed, pulling the conversation back, "I saw her talking to Hrok across the road. He was flirting with her."

"He would never flirt with a hairy woman. He finds hirsute females utterly repulsive. He made that quite clear the last time we spoke."

"Yes, and that's not all. He was obviously flirting with her - and she seemed to be lapping it up - and then the husband came out. That's when I noticed someone watching them. I only saw them out of the corner of my eye, but I think it was a woman."

"A woman?"

"I think so, but she had gone when I turned to look. Anyway, the husband joined them on the pavement and talked to Hrok in a harsh manner. His face was like thunder, that's how I know it was a harsh manner because I couldn't hear them being in the shop and the door being closed." I took a deep breath. "And then the husband began to walk away but he tripped off the path and Hrok looked very smug, and I thought then that Hrok had caused it. And then-"

"Slow down, Livitha. I can barely keep up with you."

"And then," I said a little slower, "the woman fell although it looked as though she had been pushed. But the strangest thing was her skirt. It flipped up over her knickers, almost as if it had been plucked by fingers and thrown up, if you know what I mean."

"Hrok did that?"

"No, I don't think so. He looked shocked to be honest."

"And the woman who was watching?"

"She walked away."

"She didn't stop to help?"

I shook my head. "No. The woman who had fallen came into the shop the next day. I noticed then that she had a fine growth of hair on her chin."

"And that was before the demonstration?"

"It was."

"So ... Hrok did it?" suggested Aunt Thomasin.

"Why on earth would Hrok do it?"

"So he could make a move on her," suggested Lucifer.

"And why would he do that when he says that he cannot stand hairy women?"

"He wants to make her repulsive to the husband so that he can swoop in and pick her up once she has been rejected. It's a well-known tactic of lotharios such as Hrok."

"Interesting," said Beatrice.

"It's a classic move," declared Lucifer.

"Yes, but Hrok already has six women and he complained about having that many—they tire him out. He came in for aphrodisiacs."

"Too much information, Livitha."

"Did you give him any?"

"Yes, I gave him some of Euphemia's potency potion."

Aunt Euphemia raised her brows. "Then the Slawston crones are in for a good time!"

"Euphemia!" Aunt Beatrice chided.

"Well, it does work wonderfully well. It's a potent fertility potion too."

All three aunts stared at her and then turned to me.

"You did not give him a fertility potion!"

"I ... I didn't know!"

Aunt Euphemia shook her head, holding back laughter. "The women need to take it for it to be useful that way. It just makes men more virile. It's in great demand with the village men although several did ask that I not give it out to the women. Thomas Parry has five sons and seven daughters, and the gossip is that his wife has been taking the potion since their marriage."

"And has she?"

Aunt Euphemia nodded. "Yes. She buys it in bulk. She's a passionate woman and loves babies."

Aunt Beatrice cackled.

"So, it is possible that Hrok is the cause of the plague of hairiness afflicting the housewives."

"It's possible," I said, "but I'm not sold on the motive."

Lucifer cast me a sour glare.

"There's also one thing that we are forgetting," said Aunt Euphemia.

"Which is?"

"That Livitha was trialling Thomasin's cream. That cream was from the same batch used by Livitha at the WI and at our promotional event. Livitha does not have a face full of hair." She said this with a triumphant smile.

"Oh, she does have a hairy chin. She just plucks it in the morning," said Lucifer with a sly grin. "I've watched her numerous times."

"Aunt Loveday," I said. "If you could teach me that silencing spell this evening ..."

"Certainly, dear," she replied. "In the meantime, we must discover who the mysterious bystander was."

Chapter Nineteen

With Priscilla being guarded by Old Mawde and Hegelina Fekkit in the field, I showered and dressed for work whilst ruminating on the problem of what to do with her.

"We could keep her," I suggested as I sat at the table.

My aunts eyed me with interest.

I took another sip of tea then took a bite of toast thickly spread with butter and marmalade and waited for their response.

Aunt Loveday shook her head. "She may deserve it, Livitha, but it would bring too much attention to us. She would become a missing person."

"We should wipe her memory at the very least."

Aunt Loveday looked pensive. "We shall have to wipe the memories of the entire village," she said.

"It's worse than that," Aunt Thomasin said. "The pitchfork mob will be spreading the word about Livitha's attack on the woman. Their stories about how she turned Priscilla into a goat will become a local legend."

"One we must refute. Priscilla must be released this morning, without any memory of her ordeal."

This was met with agreement among the women.

"Livitha," said Aunt Loveday, "after breakfast release Priscilla from the curse."

"I'm not sure I know how to," I said with sudden realisation. "I've only ever turned women into goats."

"Well, this is a good time to discover just how to do that," said Aunt Loveday.

She seemed unconcerned about my inability to return Priscilla to her normal form, and I took confidence from that. After finishing my breakfast, I put on my boots, fleece, and raincoat, then headed for the door picking up the pile of Priscilla's neatly folded clothes on the way out.

"We should consider a journey, sisters," I heard Aunt Euphemia say as I closed the door behind me.

With the task of confronting Priscilla ahead, I didn't dwell on Euphemia's comment and headed for the field.

Three heads poked out of the pen's glassless window as I approached the fence. Irritated bleating followed and then all three goats trotted out. Old Mawde led the way with Priscilla following and Hegelina in the rear. At one point, Priscilla darted to the left but was quickly headed off by Old Mawde and expertly herded back into line by Hegelina. The procession moved at a pace towards me.

"Livitha Winifred Erikson, I demand that you remove this annoying sack of puss from my pen!" exclaimed Old Mawde.

"I demand it too," bleated Hegelina. "She is a sour-faced and rancid oaf. I have not had one wink of sleep. She snores like a bull."

"And the windy bag farts like one too!"

"Stinking wretch!"

"Cretins!" hissed Priscilla. "I'll have you sold to the butcher and feed your innards to the pigs on Old Dave's farm!"

As the insults and demands continued between the three bickering nanny goats, I considered leaving the curse intact and face the consequences from the villagers instead. After the past few days, a belligerence was growing inside me. I had spent far too many years of my life taking abuse from people like Priscilla and Pascal. Perhaps it was time for my new-found powers to be put to good use and rectify those harms.

They'll hate us even more though.

So? They blame us for everything and want to burn us alive for a few hairs on their chins. Perhaps it is time for them to really blame us for something significant.

Like keeping one hostage as a goat.

Every call on the aether is a debt, Livitha.

Hexing from spite is only a step away from the dark side of magick.

A shiver ran through my body, and I focused on the trio of goats. Priscilla was the largest by far and her udder swung pendulum-like beneath her belly, already filled with milk. I considered milking her before removing the curse, but the thought of grasping Priscilla's teats and giving them a pull was repulsive. I brushed my hands against my jeans to rid them of the imagined sensation.

"I've come to collect her. She's to go back to the village."

"Stop off at the slaughterhouse on the way!" quipped Old Mawde.

"Tell them to gut her and throw her gizzards to the crows!" bleated Hegelina Fekkit.

"Get me out of here now," bleated Priscilla. "These goats are evil!"

Hegelina and Old Mawde cackled.

"Fat toad, I'll curse thee for a hundred years."

"Livitha!" Priscilla shrieked. "Get me out now!"

I had expected to find her cowed, but she seemed only to be consumed by rage. Only one thing saved her from another day in the pen, and that was that she hadn't made any threats towards me. I opened the gate. She ran through then darted to the left and then the right.

"Slow down," I called. "Then I'll remove the curse."

She slowed then stopped and turned to face me.

"And you'll need these," I said, holding up the pile of neatly folded clothes.

She trotted forward, head lowered. For a moment she appeared to be readying herself to charge and batter me with her satanically curled horns. Instead, she stopped several feet away and then held my gaze in a confrontational stare. "I demand that you turn me back to normal!" she spat.

"I'm going to," I replied.

"And promise never to do this again!" she demanded.

"Well, if you-"

"Promise!" she hissed.

She continued to hold my gaze and I waited for the threats to begin to flow. When they didn't, I agreed to remove the curse and suggested that she say please.

"Please!" she spat without hint of remorse.

Priscilla had always been a bully and the experience of being turned into a goat had not softened her. She remained hard and defiant.

"I promise not to turn you into a goat again on one condition," I said, unfazed by her steely gaze."

"Which is?"

"That if anyone asks, you deny that I turned you into a goat."

"But you did. Everyone saw it."

This was true, but I knew my aunts would come up with a way to deal with it. "That's the condition, take it or leave it."

"Fine!" she said.

"Good! Now, if you will stand perfectly still, I shall try and turn you back into a woman."

"Try?"

"Yes," I said, now enjoying myself. "I haven't done it before and there's a possibility that things will go wrong."

"What kind of incompetent witch are you?" Her voice was scathing.

"One that may turn you back into a woman with three legs or two noses if you don't shut up!" I retorted.

She clamped her jaws together and stood still but the defiant and sour stare remained.

Changing Priscilla back into a woman was far easier than I had imagined although my first attempt was a failure and, as she morphed, a large lump, complete with hair, began to protrude from her shoulder. I panicked but quickly recovered and turned her back into a goat then tried again. Thankfully, the second attempt was a success, and I turned my back as she dressed, hoping that all internal organs were as they should be.

Once she was dressed, I offered to give her a lift to the village, but she declined and turned towards the gate a little unsteady, her skin a deathly pallor. Satisfied that my mistake had had the unintended consequence of making her fearful of my power, I returned to the house, informed my aunts of my success, then helped dry the pots before making my way to the shop.

Priscilla had made surprising progress on her walk home and I slowed the car beside her as she strode along, pleased to see that the colour had returned to her cheeks. She puffed as she walked and ignored me at first.

I tried again to offer help. "Can I give you a lift, Priscilla?" I asked.

She mouthed something I didn't catch but given the narrowed eyes, and dog's bottom puckered mouth that followed, I guessed it was a 'No,' but without the thanks.

"Okay," I said with a smile that wasn't entirely without mirth and accelerated away from her. A quick glance in the rear-view mirror confirmed her lack of gratitude and I chuckled as she lowered her arm and middle finger. It also confirmed that she remained uncowed. I ignored the hand signal and motored into the village with the intention of putting the incident behind me and jotting down notes from the experience in order to make an entry into my grimoire later in the evening. The carbuncle on her shoulder, which had protruded enough to exhibit a pair of closed but bulging eyes, had been the result of my concentration lapsing. My thoughts had drifted for a fraction of a second to Prudence Wellwisher. Interestingly, the hair colour of the second head had matched Prudence's. Undoing curses, I realised, had to be undertaken with the greatest of care if the cursed subject was to be returned to its original state. However, I noted with interest, I now had the power to transform someone into something else just by conflating my thoughts. The realisation washed over me with a frisson of excitement followed by an enormous wave of dread. I had the power to destroy lives! The realisation was at once terrible and incredible.

The village boundary came into view, and I pushed the thoughts away and headed for the shop. As I approached, my stomach sank. Bright pink graffiti had been scrawled across the front wall and fliers stuck across the window. I pulled into the kerb and stopped in front of the shop.

There were a number of phrases written, including, 'We hate witches', and 'Burn the witches', but the one that cut at me was, 'Livitha Erikson is a witch'.

The graffiti wasn't just aimed at any witches, or even my aunts, it was personal and aimed at me! It was also a déjà vu. 'Livitha Erikson is a witch' had frequently been scrawled across desks, benches, and walls when I was at school. I suspected the same culprits this time too; those women at the WI who had once been my classmates. I couldn't blame Priscilla this time, as she had been at Haligern when the vandals had set about proclaiming their hatred.

Thankfully, apart from one woman who had walked past on the other side of the road, sunglasses and headscarf covering much of her hairy face, and Glenda Burchill who waved and smiled as she walked her dog, the village was quiet and even the tables in the café window opposite were empty. However, my cheeks stung just as badly as they had when I was ten, standing in the school yard with a group of hate-filled girls surrounding me, poking me with a stick and chanting that I was a witch, or worse, a 'smelly witch'. Fire grew in my belly and my fingers tingled.

Swaprian, Livitha. Swaprian, daughter of Soren, the ancient voices sang. *Be calm.*

"You're right," I murmured as the singsong voices lulled my fractious nerves. After taking a deep breath, I entered the shop then set about boiling a kettle of water and finding soap and a scrubbing brush. Minutes later, with a bucket filled with hot and soapy water, scrubbing brush bobbing among the bubbles, I returned outside, wet the fliers, and then began to scrub at the graffiti. Thankfully, like at school, the nasty words were written in chalk and disappeared beneath the brush. Pink suds dropped to the floor as I scrubbed the wall with vigour.

As I turned my attention to the wetted fliers, a car's engine grew loud. It slowed as it drew level and I turned to see Priscilla scowling at me from the passenger seat. The car slowed to a stop and Priscilla stepped out. The driver's door opened seconds later, and Mandy Braithwaite's head popped up above the car's roof. Her copper beard glinted in the sun. Unlike the scurrying woman who had passed only minutes ago, Mandy had her hair up in a tight ponytail. Her beard looked groomed and luxurious. A momentary thought of offering beard care products quickly vanished as Priscilla stepped towards me. Her own beard a badger-like muddy brown with grey streaks, was unflattering in comparison to Mandy's. Plus, it seemed even longer and more straggling than when she had morphed back to a woman from her goat form. As she bore down on me, I pushed away thoughts of transforming her back into a goat although I was tempted to change her into a toad. I shuddered; she would be a grotesque and hulking bull frog. Somehow, Haligern coven had to regain its good reputation in the village and throwing out more curses, no matter how well they were deserved, was not going to help.

Beneath Priscilla's glare, my heart began to beat a little faster and hysteria began to bubble. *Stand your ground!*

"Cilla! Let her be," Mandy said as Priscilla took several steps towards me.

Priscilla took no notice and threw me a hard and menacing stare, fists clenched. She remained several feet away, oppressive, Amazonian, her face ugly with hate.

Don't let her scare you into using magick. "Can I help you?" I asked as she glowered, determined not to cower or retaliate by threatening her with magick.

Mandy moved out from behind the car and tugged at Priscilla's sleeve. Her beard glinted copper in the mid-morning November sun.

"Leave it be, Cilla. Let's go back to mine and have a coffee."

Priscilla tugged her sleeve from Mandy's grip.

"Just shut up, Mandy," she said. "I'll deal with this once and for all."

"You bitch!" Mandy's face hardened and her eyes narrowed. "Leave Liv alone. You've bullied her long enough. It's your own fault she turned you into a goat."

I'm not sure what surprised me more. Priscilla's lack of fear despite being turned into a goat or that Mandy was sticking up for me.

Priscilla growled, then said, "What did you say?"

"I said, leave Liv alone. Bitch!"

In the next second, Priscilla swivelled on her toes and grabbed Mandy by the beard. "Just because you like your beard, doesn't mean she gets away with turning us into freaks."

"I didn't do anything!" I protested. "It wasn't me, or my aunts!"

"Shut it, witch!" Priscilla spat whilst retaining her grip on Mandy's beard.

"Listen to her, Cilla! It wasn't them," Mandy protested.

Beard gripped in Priscilla's fist, she gave it a slow twist. "Of course it was them!"

"It wasn't!" I added. "Leave Mandy alone, Priscilla. You're hurting her."

"Good. The silly cow needs to learn a lesson."

"You're just upset because she looks better with a beard than you do," I jibed.

Priscilla threw me a glance that was pure acid. "That's not true," she said.

"It is," retorted Mandy. "You said it wasn't fair mine was shiny and glossy and yours was straggling and dull."

"It's her inner beauty shining through," I added, unable to resist tweaking Priscilla.

I regretted my jibe instantly as she tightened the grip on Mandy's beard and began to pull.

Mandy sucked breath in through clenched teeth but didn't back down. "Liv's right. I look better than you do, and you can't stand it!" she retaliated. "You've always been the same and I'm sick of it!"

I was impressed. Despite being in pain, she was taking a stand against the domineering woman. Finally!

"And," she said, her chin now pointing skyward as Priscilla continued to pull, "I look more like a woman with a beard than you do without!"

"How dare you!" Priscilla gave the street a quick and furtive glance.

"You're very mannish even without it," Mandy added. "And ... men love me even with my beard. You're just jealous because I've got more fans than you!"

Priscilla released Mandy's beard as though it were white-hot metal then grabbed her arm. "Just get in the car," she hissed. "You're humiliating us."

Mandy had hit a nerve and I watched in startled fascination as she was bundled into the car by Priscilla. As they drove away, Priscilla's face was set to stone.

I returned my attention to the window and the sodden fliers. Before I began to scrub, I read one. It was for a meeting at the village hall to be held that afternoon. 'Purity is joy' was written in a heart shaped balloon. 'Learn how to keep your husbands pure' was printed in block capitals across the centre whilst underneath it read, 'Workshop to be led by our esteemed leader, Prudence Wellwisher. Women only.' I decided to attend.

Chapter Twenty

At five minutes to three o'clock I closed the shop and took the short walk to the village hall.

I hesitated on the step then swung the door open and was confronted by Prudence Wellwisher. At almost six foot tall, she towered over me. With her long limbs and white-blonde hair, she bore an uncanny resemblance to Hrok's 'wives' although several decades older than the forms the Slawston crones inhabited.

"How can I help you?" she asked with a pleasant and friendly smile.

"I saw the flier for this afternoon's workshop."

The slightest crease between her brow was quickly smoothed. "And you feel you have a need to attend?"

I nodded, again scrabbling through my mind for a suitable response. "I'm soon to be married. I'd like to start it off on the right foot. Agnes said that you were teaching women how to please their husbands."

"Agnes?"

I searched the room for Agnes Driscoll without success. "Agnes Driscoll, she's our cleaner's daughter. She spoke very highly of your meetings," I lied.

Prudence's eyes narrowed and seemed to search mine. Her top lip twitched. "We teach our members how to live a happy and fulfilled life with a loyal man, not how to pleasure one." She raised a brow whilst holding my gaze.

My cheeks flushed at the insinuation. "Oh! No. I didn't mean that!"

She nodded. "Purity is joy, particularly within marriage."

Was she promoting celibacy within marriage? "I'd like to know how I can make a happy marriage."

"Purity brings joy and therefore a happy marriage," she said.

"Purity is joy!" the women behind her repeated in a singsong chorus.

Nutters! "I'm interested how that can be achieved," I said, now genuinely curious.

Prudence stepped aside with a sweep of her arm. "Welcome, Livitha, dau-" She paused mid-sentence and offered me a broad smile instead. "Please, sit with us."

The women were seated on large cushions in a ring. No one spoke and only a few returned my smile of greeting as I approached.

"Sit," commanded Prudence and placed a cushion in a space between two women, then returned to her own cushion directly opposite.

Swathed in discomfort as a dozen pairs of eyes watched me, I lowered myself to sit.

"We have a newcomer who would like to join us," said Prudence. "Sisters of Purity, say hello."

"Hello," the group replied in unison.

"Please," Prudence said, smiling across the circle at me. "Introduce yourself."

"Hi," I said with a smile, scanning the faces in the circle and attempting to make eye contact with as many of the women as possible. "I'm Liv."

It was the first time that I had seen the housewives in a group since the demonstration at the Women's Institute, and their hairiness was impressive. The afflicted women had grown hair, but not your common and garden, menopause-induced, hairy lip or wispy whiskers under the chin variety. No, the village housewives had grown huge and curling moustaches, full and luxurious beards, thick and bushy eyebrows, and impressive lambchops spanning jawline to temple. Calling them hirsute was an understatement. One, with particularly dark hair that was almost black, looked wolfman-like. I shuddered. Whatever magick had befallen the poor creatures was strong.

My welcome was met by chuntering and the women looked from one to the other. A woman raised her hand as though she were at school.

"You may speak, Abby."

"Why is she here?" she asked.

Chuntering of approval followed her question.

"Let us not speak out of turn, ladies," Prudence instructed. The women grew silent.

Another woman raised her hand.

"Go ahead and speak," said Prudence.

"I would like to object to her presence."

Prudence raised a brow although I suspected it wasn't in surprise. "Pray, tell us why."

"She's the reason we're all ..." the woman swallowed, "hairy!" she spat, her voice hoarse with emotion.

Arms shot into the air, and the women looked with pleading eyes to Prudence as though they were children in a classroom desperate to be the one to answer the teacher's question.

"Sarah," Prudence said. "You may speak."

"She's a witch and she turned Priscilla into a goat!"

I couldn't deny it. I remained calm.

Prudence looked around the circle and pointed at another woman. "Clare, go ahead."

"I agree with Jane. She should not be allowed to sit among us. Look at her smooth skin! She's just come here to laugh at us!"

"I have not!" I blurted.

Noise began to bubble as the women chuntered.

Prudence held her hand in the air then turned to me. "We do not speak out of turn, Liv. Each woman has her own protected space, we do not impose ourselves upon it."

The workshop was worse than I imagined, worse than school. "So-"

Prudence raised a silencing hand. "You must raise your hand, Livitha, dear, and I will give you permission to speak. Or not."

Insufferable! How the village women put up with the controlling woman I was at a loss to understand. That they would willingly sit here and be pushed about and silenced was baffling. I searched their faces as Prudence began to speak. Only a few of the women were beardless. The rest sported beards in various stages of growth. Most were long, luxurious, full and curling but some looked partially grown whilst others were little more than a teenage boy's bum fluff. Several had regrowth in the form of stubble. One woman still had a small piece of bloodied tissue stuck to her jaw. The hairs had grown so quickly that they were poking through the tissue, which was being lifted away from her face by new growth. She noticed my stare and quickly covered her face with her scarf. As I watched the hair grow in real time, I realised the witchcraft being cast against the women was sustained and malicious, a hex.

I began to ponder the evidence I had gathered so far. The appearance of hair had come over a period of days and was not present on all of the housewives. A hypothesis began to form.

I scanned the women with renewed interest.

My breath caught as I noticed two with curling beards that hadn't been at the demonstration evening.

I grew excited.

When I spotted a woman who had been at the demonstration, had bought cream, and showed no sign of a beard, I felt confident enough to test my hypothesis. If I was correct, then Haligern coven was off the hook for the crime.

"I can prove that the cream was not the cause of the growth of hairs," I blurted, interrupting Prudence.

Several of the women sucked in their breath and all looked to Prudence for her reaction. One woman raised her hand. Prudence nodded. "You have permission to speak, Jane."

"Prove it then!" Jane spat and lowered her arm.

I began to lay out my thoughts, of how I had noticed hairy growth beneath Priscilla's chin before the demonstration, how the cream had been tested and found to contain no contaminants or combination of ingredients that could have caused hair growth, and how Lisa and Meghan sat opposite me with full beards and extensive sideburns, had neither been at

the demonstration nor purchased cream from the apothecary."
I took a deep breath. Proof of my innocence lay with my next
question. "Lisa and Meghan, have you used the anti-ageing
cream sold by Haligern Apothecary."

Meghan raised her hand. "I have not. I use Swan's
moisturiser."

It all hung on Lisa's answer.

"Lisa you may answer," Prudence allowed.

Lisa shook her head. "No. I haven't used the cream either."

"So, in conclu-"

Prudence raised a silencing palm. I gritted my teeth and
waited for permission.

"Go ahead, Liv."

"So, in conclusion, the cream was not to blame for the
hairy growth on Meghan or Lisa's face. So, it can't be what had
made the rest of the ladies hairy either."

Prudence nodded. "That is sound logic."

I remembered a beardless Glenda Burchill walking past the
shop with her dog. "And! And Glenda does not have a beard.
She was my model. That proves the cream is not to blame."

"It proves nothing!" spat Jane. "You're a witch. You could
have hexed us instead."

What was it going to take for them to believe me? Hope
began to fade. I was never going to win.

"She's a witch," Jane continued. "She could have hexed us!"
she repeated.

"Hsst!"

I turned to stare at Prudence. She had reprimanded Jane
with the traditional way witches expressed deep dissatisfaction
and I remembered her stilted welcome, she had nearly given my

full name, Livitha, daughter of Soren. She knew who I was and what I was which meant she had to be a witch herself!

Taken aback, I was overwhelmed with the need to leave the hall. I raised a hand. Priscilla gave her permission for me to speak. "Apologies, ladies, but I've just remembered an important engagement." I looked at my watch as though to prove it. "It has been lovely to meet you." My tone was completely disingenuous, but I was past caring and rose from the cushion, surprised at the effort it took to get off the floor. "I'd love to see you at the apothecary sometime soon. We have lots of creams and salves for many ailments." I was rambling, but my desire to leave the room, and the presence of Prudence Wellwisher, had become intense.

Prudence considered me with a hard gaze and a fixed smile as the women watched me leave in silence. I strode to the door, swung it open, and burst out into the fresh air.

Prudence is a witch!

It could be coincidence. Ordinary people hiss, don't they?

Do they?

I don't know!

I returned to the shop with the thoughts churning in my mind and closed the door behind me with a sigh of relief. The warmth of the rooms enveloped me along with the scent of the myriad elixirs, lotions, and potions, and I breathed them in as a calmative for my ragged nerves, then hurried to the kitchen to make myself a cup of tea. I placed a single drop of Aunt Thomasin's elixir into the pot then let the tea leaves seep as my thoughts whirred.

Prudence is a witch!

Stop. You don't know that. Just think things through.

I took a sip of tea and began to order my thoughts. Firstly, it was now without a doubt that Aunt Thomasin's cream was not to blame. Secondly, it was also evident that someone had cast a hex against some – not all – of the village housewives and that they had used strong magick. Was it just strong or dark magick? That was another avenue of enquiry. And thirdly, Prudence Wellwisher – stupid name – could very possibly be a witch! One of us but hiding her true nature behind a weird façade?

In that moment, I made it a top priority to discover exactly who she was. Other questions came to mind and, to help clarify my thoughts, I jotted down some notes about the woman:

Prudence Wellwisher (fake name!)

1. Where does she live?
2. Where has she come from?
3. Who does she know in the village?
4. What is known of the Purity Revival cult?
5. How long has the cult been running? Did she set it up?
6. Is she a witch?
7. What is her real name?
8. Did she cast a hex on the women? Motive?

As I scribbled down my thoughts, an idea struck, and I looked up from my fevered jottings. That was it! Prudence was a witch, and she was drawing energy from the local housewives by turning them into acolytes. But for what purpose? Was she dabbling in dark magick and using that energy to conjure darker forces? If so, that would mean a sacrifice was needed.

"No!" I blurted as my thoughts clarified. If she was dabbling in dark magick, was she gathering the women to offer as a sacrifice—a very hairy sacrifice. I scribbled down these conclusions with a trembling hand, then followed it with

- Note: check for existence of dark magick rituals that require hairy women.

Pleased with my progress, I poured myself a cup of tea, added an extra drop of calmative, then enjoyed the soothing sensation as the edge of my tension receded. A vague thought that I'd had rather a lot of the calming elixir of late and that it could be addictive was quickly lost as I returned to thoughts of Prudence.

I returned to my jottings with a final flourish:

- URGENT! Discover the true identity and nature of Prudence 'stupid name' Wellwisher ASAP!

For the remainder of the afternoon, I paced at the front of the shop, keeping an eye on the street outside for sign of Prudence. At five o'clock, I turned the sign to closed and dimmed the lights in the shop allowing me to see the street more clearly. At five fifteen the women began filtering out of the village hall. I grabbed my hat and coat and left by the back door then made my way down the passage between the apothecary and the next door shop and onto the street. Darkness had descended and the passageway was in deep shadow. To make sure I was undetectable, I enveloped myself in a hazing spell that would obscure my figure and help me blend into the surroundings.

Minutes passed and then Prudence appeared on the steps of the village hall. I waited until she had walked past the café and reached the end of the road then stepped out of the passage, following her at a distance.

Only once did Prudence look back as she walked home, and I quickly jumped into the shadows despite the hazing spell.

She made her way from the village centre to ever narrowing lanes until she reached the gate of a small cottage. I recognised it immediately as the cottage inhabited, until recently, by the crone Hetty Quinelle, who had fled the village as soon as news that her boss, Millicent, the child-thieving dark witch, had been caught and destroyed.

With my suspicions confirmed, I returned to Haligern cottage and my aunts.

Chapter Twenty-One

"I think Prudence Wellwisher is a witch," I said as we stood in the kitchen. "And the cream is innocent!"

"What draws you to that conclusion?"

"Firstly, she hissed at one of the women in the purity workshop-"

This drew murmurs from my aunts.

"That is interesting," said Aunt Beatrice, "but inconclusive. Do you have any other evidence?"

"Yes. She is staying in Hetty Quinelle's cottage."

"Ah!"

"That seals it as far as I am concerned."

"Indeed, sisters," said Aunt Beatrice. "Hetty would never allow her cottage to be inhabited by a normie."

"A normie?" asked Euphemia.

"Yes, it's what we call the folk who don't have magical powers and are unaware of the other worlds that lie within and without our own."

Aunt Thomasin shook her head. "Well, I suppose it fits."

"Yes, they are normal, hence 'normie.'"

"I see."

"So we are in agreement that we believe Prudence to be a witch."

My aunts nodded.

"She has taken Hetty's cottage. Only another witch would be offered the cottage."

"One that has only just been vacated, and one that is still chock to the rafters with Hetty's belongings."

"Then she must have permission," stated Aunt Loveday. "Which is troubling given what we know of Hetty Quinelle."

"Unless she's a squatter."

Murmurs of agreement passed among my aunts.

"She didn't take anything?" asked Aunt Euphemia.

"Very little," said Aunt Thomasin. "I assume she took her grimoire and little else, given that she fled the village in a moonlit flit."

"How do you know it's full of her stuff?"

"I looked in through the windows. Upstairs and downstairs are all filled with her belongings. She was a very neat and tidy person. Even her bed was made."

"She was very active in the village."

"Yes, and not for any good intention either."

This was followed by murmurs of agreement.

"I know of no witch by the name of Prudence Wellwisher," stated Aunt Loveday.

"Me neither."

"We must discover who Prudence is."

Again, the suggestion was followed by murmurs of agreement.

"Whoever she is, she is not one of ours."

"Or she's using a false name," Lucifer offered. "Has it not occurred to you learned crones that the name Prudence Wellwisher is a little ridiculous."

"Actually, that is exactly what I thought when I first heard it," I said.

"Then why have you not acted on that information? Tsk, tsk, Livitha, and I thought that you were progressing in your craft."

"I am," I countered.

"Not nearly fast enough," he said with a tone of disdain. "And anyway, I can assure you that she is a witch."

"How do you know that."

"I've seen her practicing magic," he said then licked his paw.

"And?" demanded Aunt Loveday.

"And she's very good at it."

"Anything else, Lucifer?"

"And she has a familiar."

"Ah!"

"So, she is a witch, but one here under false pretenses."

"Yes," replied Lucifer.

"So, what's her name?"

"That I don't know."

"But surely you have been talking with her familiar?"

"Indeed, but I have been unable to garner a name."

"So, your seductive talents have failed you this time."

Lucifer slapped his tail against the floorboards. "My seductive talents never fail me."

"They seem to have this time," I quipped, "if you don't know the familiar's name."

"That is because I would not seduce *him*! *He* being a *male* of the species." He tapped his tail against the floorboards in irritation. "And anyway, I am loyal. Ophelia ..." he let out a deep sigh. "There is only her!"

"Fair enough," I said, remembering his ardour for Hrok's familiar, a particularly stunning example of a Norwegian Forest cat with glossy black fur and huge and bright green eyes, "but can't you have a friendly chat and discover who his mistress is?"

"A familiar never betrays his mistress," Lucifer said, "and Goubert-"

"French!" said Beatrice with a nod of her head.

"And Goubert-"

"Anglo-Norman, Bea," corrected Aunt Loveday. "Remember Goubert d'Auffay. He came across the channel with Guillaume le Bâtard."

Beatrice's brow pulled together. "Oh, yes! My error. Anglo-Norman. Continue."

Lucifer stared for several moments at Aunt Beatrice, then said. "As I was saying, Goubert ... is as loyal as they come."

"Meaning that you've failed at gleaning any information from him," said Aunt Thomasin.

I thought this was a little harsh. "If he's very loyal, like Lucifer," I said, "then we can only respect him for that." This garnered a look of surprised appreciation from Lucifer.

"That is correct, Mistress," he said, then sat in regal disdain with his eyes closed.

"So now we know that Prudence is, without doubt, a witch disguising her true identity and instigating a strange, puritanical cult."

"And her familiar is of the Norman bloodlines."

"Indeed," said Lucifer.

"Which means?"

"Which means that if we can narrow down who the familiar belongs to, we will discover exactly who Prudence is and why she is in the village. There are not many familiars named Goubert."

"If that's his real name," I said.

Lucifer growled. "Once again you insult me!"

"What? How can I have insulted you?"

"A familiar never lies to another familiar! It is part of our code of honour."

I wanted to retaliate and ask, 'what code of honour?', but decided against it as I noticed Lucifer's claws extending from his furry paw as he held it up to lick. He was angry, and I did not want to be used as a pincushion by a vengeful cat for however many days, perhaps weeks, he decided my punishment should last for. "Of course," I said, restraining a tone of sarcasm. "I apologise."

He sniffed. "Apology accepted."

Chapter Twenty-Two

After our discoveries, we spent the evening going over all the evidence and I went to bed with my head filled with questions and a burning desire to discover just who Prudence really was. I slept badly, and with Lucifer's nagging voice ringing in my ear, I rose early. My aunts were already in the kitchen and the fire was being lit as I entered. They too had slept badly, and Aunt Beatrice was even more doom-filled than before.

"The dreams I've had, sisters," she complained. "After the last one, I refused to sleep."

"All will be well, Bea," Aunt Euphemia soothed. "It's just the time of year."

"And a hex is upon the village, and they accuse us of it. And a witch is drumming up a bizarre cult too! Tumult is in the air. I feel it as though it were thunder."

"I'm going to the shop early," I declared as my aunts continued to talk about the impending doom they felt as an oppressive cloud.

"But it's still dark!" Aunt Beatrice said, looking to the closed curtains as though to confirm it.

"I know, but I'm too agitated to stay inside. I need to be doing something."

"You can dry up the pots," she offered.

"I'll wash and dry up tonight," I compromised. "If that's alright with you. It's just that I woke up with such an intense need to leave the house ... I can't explain it."

"It is her! She who cannot be named. It is her evil worming its way among us—again."

"Hush!" reprimanded Aunt Euphemia. "The atmosphere in here is bad enough as it is. Look at poor Livitha, running away from the cottage because of it all."

"I'm not run-"

Aunt Euphemia raised a hand. "It's completely understandable, Livitha. I'd like to run away too. I hate this time of year. If only it were not so." She sighed then turned her attention to the fire and placed another piece of kindling among the scrunched paper.

"I am beginning to think it would be a good idea to have some time away," said Aunt Thomasin. Benny squawked from his perch on the curtain pole as though in agreement.

"That's the second time I've heard you talk of going on a journey," I said. "Are you planning something."

Glances passed between my aunts.

"Not really," Aunt Euphemia replied. "Although I do feel the need for a change of scenery." She turned to the pantry and opened the door. "Time away would help the villagers forget."

"Forget?" I asked.

Aunt Beatrice wafted dismissive hand. "Take no notice, Livitha. She gets itchy feet sometimes. A holiday would be good. We haven't had one in decades."

The fire began to crackle, steam began to rise from the kettle, and my desire to leave became intense. "I'll get off now," I said.

"Well, it is unusually early," said Aunt Beatrice, "and you haven't had any breakfast, but if you feel the need to go, then so be it."

"Something is drawing her outside," said Aunt Thomasin. "Take great care, Livitha. Our needs are not always to be met without sacrifice."

Grumbles of agreement passed between my aunts.

"Is she being drawn out, do you think?"

"It is possible," replied Aunt Thomasin.

"An ill wind doth blow," stated Aunt Beatrice in a gloomy voice. "It is her influence, I tell you!" The air above her crackled.

"Pah! Ignore her, Livitha," said Aunt Thomasin with a clap of her hands. "Go to the shop early. Get some fresh air. It will clear your head."

"Thanks," I said. "I think that's all it is—I just need a clear head for thinking."

I left the cottage with the sky still dark and stars sparkling above me. As I made my way through the winding lanes on the way to the village, the sun not yet risen, I noticed fire in the distance. It appeared to be coming from a field. As I drew closer, I picked up the scent of smoke. Sometimes teenagers would set fires, enjoying the excitement of making a bonfire, and usually it came to nothing. There had also been a recent incident of a stolen car being set alight. I motored in the direction of the fire curious as to what could be causing it. My own car had caught alight only a few months ago and I needed to check if help were needed.

I pushed the accelerator down and increased my speed following the road whilst keeping the fire in view. As I grew close, I could see that a tree was ablaze. There was no sign of a car with its engine on fire, or a burned-out wreck destroyed by vandals. I pulled over to the verge and made my way into the field. A cackle in the distance stopped me in my tracks and I searched into the darkness. The laugh had sounded as though it came from across the field. As I turned from the field towards the fire, I saw that the tree's trunk was on fire and higher up, just out of reach of the flames was a board. 'Witch' was written in red capitals.

For one dreadful moment, I thought that someone had burned a witch alive and then realised that it must be an effigy, perhaps the one made for the Night of Good Fires stolen by local teenagers and burned. I breathed an intense sigh of relief. "The villagers will be unhappy," I muttered as I took several steps towards the burning tree. Fire licked at the hedgerow and had begun to reach the upper branches. With no one around, I decided to try and put it out with magick.

I closed my eyes, sank into my mind and waited for the voices to speak. Within seconds, they began to whisper, and I listened with intent. Holding my arms out, palms flat, the skin on my hands grew cold whilst fizzing with prickles of energy. The energy stung, building up to a crescendo of pain until I flung my hands out. Ice cold sparks flew and a wave of frost, white and shimmering, enveloped the burning tree like a cloud of dry ice. The fire sizzled and the cloud vanished. Flames sputtered and reignited. Once again, I threw out the ice-cold energy to smother the tree. *Become as nought* "Naþiht geþurþe." The flames receded, sputtered, then disappeared. Embers floated orange against the black night.

Relief flooded me as the magick dissipated. "That was intense," I said then rubbed my hands together, clenching them to clear the last of the magick.

Holding out the palm of my hand, I lit a witch light the size of a football and approached the tree. The light gave out a yellow glow. *Brighten* "Beorhtnan" I commanded. The light grew bright, illuminating the tree and the figure tied to its centre.

As the scene became clear, I stalled. The figure roped to the tree was not an effigy of a witch, nor a leftover guy from Bonfire Night. It was a woman, or what was left of a woman, and from the grotesque contortions of her face, she had been burned alive. The drab beard with its streaks of grey remained miraculously, magically, intact.

"Priscilla!" I gasped, then turned to retch.

I retched several times, walking away from the horror of the tree and towards my car. I noticed a petrol cannister and pulled it from the hedgerow, holding it up as headlights caught me in their glare. Seconds later a door slammed.

"What are you doing?" a man's voice growled. "What the very hell do you think you're doing in my field?"

I held the petrol cannister can up, caught in the lights, my senses on overload simultaneously realising that I could have contaminated the crime scene, smudged the killer's fingerprints and incriminated myself. Only the other day, when I had threatened to kill Priscilla, I had done it in front of more than a dozen witnesses.

The farmer shone torchlight in my face. "The witch!" he hissed. "What are you doing here burning down my trees?" He moved the torchlight onto the tree.

"It's Priscilla," I said as another wave of nausea hit. "She's dead!"

The torchlight returned to my face. "You've killed her?" he questioned then strode towards the tree. "You've killed her!" This time the words were an accusation.

"No! I found her. I saw the fire."

The man gagged, bending over to retch.

A chill had fallen, and the tree smouldered in the cold air. He straightened, glanced my way, then began to move slowly towards the car.

"I didn't do it!" I called.

"No, of course you didn't," he said. His tone was placatory but laced with fear. He moved slowly at first, one eye on me, then ran, throwing himself into his car. The engine started and tyres squealed as he sped away, his taillights disappearing as he rounded a bend.

As I stood in the field, my back to the tree, I remembered his face. He had been at the cottage with the mob of villagers. He had witnessed my assault on Priscilla. He had heard the threats.

"So, now what do we do, Mistress?"

"Now you turn up!" I said as Lucifer appeared in front of me.

"It does smell obnoxious, although there is a taint of roast por-."

"Don't say it, Lucifer!" I warned. "Now is not the time for your supercilious nonsense. A woman has been killed."

"And by you!"

"Of course, it wasn't me."

"That's what they will think, though. You were the first on the scene. Were you the last to see her alive."

"I wasn't."

"They will presume that you were. And then there is the issue of your fingerprints being all over the petrol cannister used to douse her. Add that the threats of murder heard by dozens of villagers ... You had motive and they have reason to believe that you carried out your threats."

"I know how it looks, Lucifer," I snapped. "You don't need to tell me!"

"Then my advice remains the same."

"Which is?"

"Discover who did it and clear your name. And if I were you, I'd do it before the Night of Good Fires. I have a terrible feeling about that night this year and my senses never let me down."

He disappeared into the night leaving me holding the cannister with the nauseatingly acrid stench of Priscilla in my nostrils.

Chapter Twenty-Three

Traumatised, and with the sun now rising, I returned to the Haligern cottage. The air crackled as I entered and the lights lining the hallway dimmed. Several flared then extinguished.

Chatter from the kitchen floated into the hallway and I stalled. The image of Priscilla Dedman roped to the tree was seared on my mind. The farmer thinks I killed her! He'll be telling the police right now. They'll be here to arrest me at any minute! Oh, why did we make that cream? None of this would have happened, if we hadn't!

The voices in the kitchen had grown quiet. Footsteps tacked towards the door and then it swung open. Soft light from the oil lamps burning within, fell onto the hallway's tiled floor. I stepped back into the shadows.

"Livitha Winifred Erikson, come into the kitchen." Aunt Beatrice's tone was terse, and I obeyed without thought.

Five pairs of eyes rested on me as I stood in the doorway.

"What have you done?" Aunt Beatrice demanded.

"I'm sure it is noth-"

"Hsst! Let the child speak, Thomasin. She has something to tell us. Something dreadful. I heard her speak of it."

"You really shouldn't list-"

167

Aunt Thomasin stopped speaking as Aunt Beatrice raised a palm towards her.

"Tell us!" Aunt Beatrice demanded.

The tension in the house had been building over the last days and now each of my aunts seemed on edge. Even Aunt Loveday, usually the least skittish and most laid back, looked at me with apprehension. The impending festival where the effigy of a witch would be burned once more in celebration of the village overcoming the evil Hetty Yikkar was hanging over them like a dark and tumultuous cloud.

"Priscilla Dedman is dead!" I blurted. "She was burned alive tied to a tree. The farmer thinks I did it!"

"And she was overheard threatening to kill Priscilla!" gasped Aunt Euphemia.

Aunt Thomasin swayed.

"It is Hetty's doing!" Aunt Beatrice hissed, scouring the corners of the room. "Loveday you must cast another protective spell around the cottage. We must all cast protective spells. Oh, I fear something dreadful is coming."

"I think it is already here," Lucifer drawled. "The farmer saw Livitha with a can of petrol in her hand as she stood gloating over Priscilla's body. It was burned to a crisp. It had the odour of roast por-"

"Thank you, Lucifer. Please do not go into details."

"Oh, but the details are good!" he insisted.

"Desist, Lucifer!" Aunt Loveday demanded.

Lucifer threw me a scowl as a surrogate for Loveday then began to lick his paw. "Also, he probably saw her put out the fire with her magick!" He spat the last word.

"Oh! And so close to the Night!"

"Hush, Beatrice. Enough of this fearmongering. Livitha did not burn Priscilla Dedman to death." She turned her attention to me, catching my eyes. "Did you?"

I shook my head. "No, but does that matter? They will think I'm guilty."

"I can see the papers now. "Burned Alive! Frumpy woman sets fire to childhood bully."

"Thank you, Lucifer."

"Roasted! Middle-aged frump takes revenge on glamorous enemy."

"They would not print that!" Aunt Euphemia said.

"They might."

"They wouldn't. The headlines are not catchy enough."

"Envious frump burns glamorous bully alive!"

"Enough!"

"As you like. Anyway, back to me. It being breakfast time ..."

Without thought, I took a bottle of port from the counter and poured him a saucerful then filled his bowl with several chunks of salmon.

"I vote that Livitha burns her enemies at the stake more often," Lucifer purred as he lapped at the port.

I gave a martyred sigh. "They'll be here to arrest me."

"They will want to question you, obviously. But once you explain what happened, I doubt they'll arrest you."

"She will be arrested on suspicion of murder."

"If I hadn't given that demonstration at the WI none of this would have happened. Priscilla would be alive right now."

The room grew silent.

"Is that an admission of guilt, Livitha?" Aunt Loveday asked.

"No! I just mean … one thing leads to another. If I hadn't fought with Priscilla …"

"Then what?" asked Aunt Euphemia. "I don't believe her murder had anything to do with you. How could it?"

Lucifer's nagging voice returned to my memory. "We have to discover who Prudence Wellwisher is. She has something to do with this. I am sure!"

"We know that she's a witch," said Aunt Loveday. "But what makes you think she has anything to do with Priscilla's murder?"

"I noted it down!" I reached into my bag. "Here! I stabbed at the page. I was thinking everything through earlier. Why has she set up this cult? Why is she drawing the housewives to her? Why is she causing problems in the village."

"And what answer did you come to?"

"That she's drawing them to her as acolytes, possibly to use in dark magick sacrifices! It's here. Written down. She burned Priscilla alive as a sacrifice. She's dabbling in dark magick!"

"That is a very serious accusation to make against a witch."

"I know! But a woman has been burned alive. We must find out who she really is and why she is here."

My aunts looked from one to the other, the tension in the room growing intense.

"We should go to the Council of Witches. They will have a record of all familiars. There can't be many that go by the name of Goubert," I said.

"And what good will that do?"

"Then we'll know who she is!"

"First, you must discover who killed Priscilla. You can't just accuse a witch of dark magick sacrifices without proper evidence of guilt," schooled Aunt Loveday.

"But a woman has been burned alive!" I repeated. "And Prudence Wellwisher could be involved."

"*She* is involved in this," said Aunt Beatrice. "I feel it in my bones." She shook her head. "She could be listening-."

"No, Beatrice!" Aunt Loveday interjected. "Don't say it."

"I doubt very much that *she* would be hiding in the corners of the kitchen, Beatrice," Aunt Thomasin said with a sigh.

"She could have transmogrified into a spider. Her essence could be in the very webs that they spin!"

"That's stuff and nonsense, Beatrice!" Aunt Loveday scolded. "The woman is dead. D. E. A. D."

"I know how to spell the word, Loveday. You do not need to be facetious!"

"I'm not, but I am heartily sick of your histrionics! Het-She who shall not be named cannot harm us."

"No! But her descendants could!"

"Does she have descendants?" I asked.

"Of course, she does! She is a Yikkar. I can count a dozen descendants off the top of my head."

"Such as."

"Well ... there's Grimlock, for a start."

"He's hardly likely to be seeking vengeance against us," said Aunt Loveday.

Her words piqued my interest. "Why would Hetty's descendants want to take vengeance against us?" I asked.

Aunt Loveday caught my gaze then quickly looked away.

She had a secret! They all had a secret and it involved Hetty Yikkar. "There's something you're not telling me," I said. "If my life is in danger, then I have the right to know about it."

"Put the kettle on, Beatrice. We shall have a cup of tea and then tell you the story of-"

"The grim and grisly death of she who shall not be named!" said Aunt Beatrice with a final scan into the shadows of the kitchen before turning to the stove to remove the kettle.

A bubble of hysterical laughter caught in my throat, and I snorted.

"It is no laughing matter," scolded Aunt Thomasin. "The woman was evil!"

"And that evil ended with her demise," Aunt Euphemia said.

"Yes, her grisly and unfortunate demise," said Aunt Beatrice.

Minutes later we were seated at the table with the tea brewing in its pot at the centre. The air crackled. Each of my aunts looked strained and Aunt Beatrice's hair, though pulled back into a bun had come loose and become untidy. Her hand trembled as she reached for the pot to pour out the tea. Aunt Loveday placed a hand upon hers. "I'll be mother, Bea."

After the tea was poured, Aunt Loveday began the story. Hetty Yikkar, she said, had moved into the village after which a series of unfortunate events befell the villagers. Crops began to fail, and rumours spread that Hetty Yikkar was sowing bitter herbs in the fields, conjuring devils, and fornicating with the priest. When a child went missing, they blamed her and declared she was a witch.

"But she was a witch, so they were right," I said.

"Yes, she was a witch."

"And was she guilty."

Aunt Loveday nodded. "Yes, she was guilty of most, if not all, of the charges laid against her. Worst of all though, was that the villagers began to turn on us. They accused us of being witches too and we began to fear for our lives."

"What did you do?" I asked, enthralled.

Chapter Twenty-Four

"When we confirmed that she was dabbling in dark magick, we helped the villagers to capture her."

"And they burned her at the stake!"

"But not before her poison grimoires were lost, scattered around the earth and hidden."

"You helped the villagers burn her at the stake?" I asked, unable to keep the shock from my voice.

Aunt Loveday nodded. "It was the only way. She was far too powerful for us to confront."

"And they burned her in the marketplace and have been celebrating her execution every year since."

"Yes! Since 1487. But do you know what is worse?" said Aunt Euphemia with dramatic flair.

I shook my head. "I'm not sure what could be worse than being burned alive at the stake."

"Her cursed grimoires were stolen!" she exclaimed. A flash of fear flickered in her eyes. "The evil within their pages is out there waiting to be found and when they are ... Oh, Loveday, we did a terrible thing!"

"We did what we had to do. The loss of the grimoires was an ... unintended consequence of those actions."

"It was a disaster!" blurted Aunt Beatrice. "I have been learning at the Academy just how powerful and dangerous they are. Did you know that after all these years they remain lost. Sometimes their magick is used and it surfaces, and the Keeper seeks them out, but they remain lost."

"After all these centuries, Arne has not gathered them together?"

"He has found some, but not all. And the curse within them is still strong."

"Who is Arne?" I asked.

"Arne Lothbrok ... oh, he was a fine and handsome warrior," sighed Aunt Euphemia. "Such a ... well, such a man!"

Aunt Beatrice tittered.

"Oh, Livitha, the times we had together ... until Mawde ..." she clenched her jaws. "But I shall say no more. What has been, has been."

"And what is done, is done!" said Aunt Loveday.

"Indeed," said Aunt Beatrice with a sigh. "He was very handsome though and so ... virile."

"Beatrice!"

"I know, I know," she said wafting a hand in Aunt Loveday's direction. "But he was so well-suited to Euphemia. They could have married you know," she said with a glance in my direction, "and would have been if Mawde had not interfered." She looked with a sour frown towards the kitchen window and the field beyond where Old Mawde slept.

Aunt Loveday sighed. "I would rather not remember if you don't mind, sisters."

"I agree," said Aunt Euphemia. "It only makes my longing worse."

"Pah! Do not tell me you're still lovesick for Arne Lothbrok," said Aunt Thomasin. "There have been many lovers since him, some that you liked even better."

I sat entranced by their reminiscences. They had led such fantastical lives, much of which was still hidden from me. As the room grew quiet, my thoughts turned to the housewives and Prudence. "Could whoever hexed the villagers have one of the grimoires? Have they used dark magick to hex the housewives?"

Aunt Loveday shook her head. "I have considered it – not the cursed grimoires, but the hex itself – and no, I do not believe it is formed from dark magick. It is a simple enough spell and carries no long-lasting damage."

"Apart from the housewives' pride, perhaps," added Aunt Thomasin.

"And it could damage their marriages."

"And it has given us untold trouble and now people are petitioning for us to be thrown out of the village and burning women alive!"

I was more convinced than ever that we needed to get to uncover the true identity of Prudence Wellwisher. "You know, I've been thinking about timelines, and when things began to happen it was around the same time that Prudence Wellwisher arrived in the village."

"She certainly seems to be stirring up the local population."

"That's when they began to take against Hrok. Mrs. Driscoll said that the petition against him was started before Bonfire Night."

"And she arrived two weeks beforehand."

"Which is when she began her proselytizing. Agnes told Mrs. Driscoll that she offered her first workshop on the third of November."

"Her message spread quickly then."

"And with fervour, a religious-like dedication to the rituals and a deep dislike of anyone who didn't follow her teachings."

"Purity is joy. Pah!"

"They seem to have had a particular impact on Hrok," mulled Aunt Loveday. "And I find it most peculiar that a witch should turn up in Haligern, live here under a false name, and stir up the local women with an almost religious and puritanical fervour."

"It is most peculiar," Aunt Euphemia agreed.

"Do you think that stirring up hate towards Hrok could be deliberate?"

"I am beginning to wonder if that might be the case. Who began the petition against Hrok?"

"Priscilla," I said. "She was like a demented dog about forcing Hrok and the Slawston crones out of the village."

"Yes, and not for being their true selves, for the identities they have chosen to inhabit – a debonair man and his six glamorous concubines."

"So, they haven't taken against them for witchcraft. As far as the villagers are aware, Hrok is a playboy and the crones his paramours," Aunt Beatrice said.

"So, they do not know that Hrok is a sorcerer, and the crones are witches."

"Correct," I said.

"But if Prudence Wellwisher is really a witch, which seems probable, then she would know that truth. We cannot hide ourselves easily from one another."

"I didn't know that the Slawston sisters were witches until I saw them transform."

"No, but you knew the moment you met them, didn't you."

"Well, I could tell that something was off," I said.

"It is a conundrum," said Aunt Thomasin, "but what are we to do?"

I wasn't sure what to suggest and given the tension among my aunts, didn't want to burden them. "I was considering asking the Council of Witches to give us some advice."

Four pairs of eyes gave me a hard stare.

"We do not want the Council of Witches involved in this," Aunt Loveday stated.

"If they discover our part in Hetty's demise ..."

"Indeed, Thomasin," said Loveday. "We shall have to deal with the problem ourselves. I have every faith in you, Livitha, to get to the bottom of this mystery."

A wretched and yowling howl brought our conversation to a hard stop, and we all turned to Lucifer. His eyes were wide and every hair on his body stood on end.

"What in the name of Thor-"

"Time is running out." Lucifer's drawling voice was uncharacteristically deep.

A shiver of energy, cold and dank, whipped through the kitchen, blowing at my aunts' skirts.

"Hsst!"

The familiar's eyes were glazed. "I have been trying to warn you ... and yet still you do not listen."

"What is he saying?" Aunt Beatrice whispered and clung to Aunt Euphemia.

The room was deathly silent as we all stared at the cat. He stood frozen with his hackles raised. "Mistress Livitha is in mortal danger," he continued in the strange and dour voice. "She must discover who hexed the housewives or she will join Hetty at the stake. So it has been foretold."

Aunt Beatrice yelped, swayed and began to fall as Lucifer yowled then fled the kitchen.

"Bea!"

Though startled, I swung into action and dashed to save Aunt Beatrice's fall, scooping her into my arms. My inner magical strength rallied, and I walked across to the chair by the fire, holding the tiny and unconscious woman like a child. Aunt Thomasin wafted a cloth above her whilst Aunt Euphemia searched the shelves for smelling salts.

She murmured against my shoulder.

"She's alive!" Aunt Thomasin exclaimed.

"Of course she is," said Aunt Loveday. "Beatrice is as tough as old boots."

Holding her slight frame in my arms, she didn't seem to be as tough as old boots. "She passed out," I said. "This is all getting too much for her."

"It's being a worry wart that's doing it," said Aunt Euphemia to murmurs of agreement. "And I can't find the smelling salts!"

"Make a pot of tea, Euphemia," Aunt Loveday instructed then rubbed her fingers beneath Aunt Beatrice's nose. Dust rose in a twist of black particles as sparks crackled between her fingers. The air smelled of burning tyres. Aunt Beatrice jerked in my arms as the acrid particles slipped into her nostrils then batted Aunt Loveday's hands away.

A collected sigh of relief passed among us.

"Beatrice, are you alright?"

"You swooned, dear."

"She could have crumpled onto the floor with such a thud if it weren't for Livitha. Are we sure nothing is broken?"

"I have no pain, dear sisters, though thank you for your concern."

"Livitha saved you. She was very quick to act," praised Aunt Euphemia as she poured boiling water into the pot.

"Such a good child," said Aunt Beatrice with a weak voice.

"Poor Bea. The last few weeks have been a torment for her. She never does very well at this time of year."

"In future we must not mention she who shall not be named and then we can forget about the nasty business."

"It is the pact we made all those years ago."

Aunt Loveday nodded. "It is only the villagers who do not let us forget."

"Can we not make them forget?"

Aunt Loveday shook her head. "It would take too much of our energy for us to make an entire village forget a day that is imprinted on their memories."

"Then we are to suffer this day for ever more."

"Perhaps we can spend these months travelling? We used to travel—before. Could we do it again?"

"I should like to travel," I said, remembering the farmer's look of horrified accusation as he had run back to his car after seeing Priscilla tied to the tree. A police car was probably winding its way to the cottage at this very moment. "Garrett!" I blurted. "I forgot to call him. What if the police arrest me?"

Chapter Twenty-Five

It was agreed that Garrett would know what to do and I was instructed to call him and explain exactly what had happened. As I stepped outside of the cottage to speak to him privately, I heard the whining of an ambulance and police cars in the distance. The farmer had reported the murder. They would be coming for me next!

I stood beside the fence. Old Mawde and Hegelina Fekkit eyed me with disdain.

"Garrett!"

"Liv."

His tone was cold. He already knew.

"Something terrible has happened."

"But not as terrible as *will* happen!" Old Mawde said. She had sidled up to the fence as I waited for him to answer.

"Oh, shut up!" I said.

"Liv? You want me to shut up?"

"No! Not you."

"Where are you?" he asked with a professional edge to his voice.

"At home. Sorry! Old Mawde distracted me," I threw a glare at the cursed goat.

"Twill be home no longer, Livitha Winifred Erikson, if you tarry here longer, you raddled old hag!"

I turned away from the malicious goat. "Priscilla Dedman has been murdered, but I didn't do it!" I blurted.

There was silence on the other end of the line until he said, "I'm on my way."

"Are you coming to arrest me?"

"No! I can't be part of the investigation. Our relationship is a conflict of interests."

"So, they think I did it?"

"Liv, you have been reported as present at the scene. The farmer-"

"He thinks I did it!" My voice held a touch of hysteria.

"He'll be making a statement. I don't know much more than that. Like I said, I won't be part of the case."

"There are police sirens and an ambulance! I can hear them."

Old Mawde cackled. "You won't be needing an ambulance once you're burned to a crisp!" The last word was spat with delighted malice.

"Shut up!" I hissed.

"Liv?"

"Sorry! It's Old Mawde, she's being vile."

"As usual," Garrett stated. "She's a rotten old goat. Ignore her. And Liv ..."

"Yes?"

"Just stay calm until I get there, okay?"

"You've got to help clear my name!"

"I'm five minutes away. Just stay calm."

"You believe me, don't you?"

There was a moment of silence before he answered. "Yes, of course I do. See you in a minute."

He ended the call and the watery flip that had turned in my stomach as he'd said 'of course I do' without conviction, became nauseous.

"What ails you, dear?" asked Old Mawde. Her voice was almost tender.

"Oh, nothing."

"It's not nothing, I can tell."

"It's just that a woman was murdered."

"And they think that you did it?"

"Well, the farmer does, but not my aunts."

"Of course, your aunts will always be loyal, but your lover ... he's unsure ... isn't he."

I gave a deep and martyred sigh. "I'm ... I'm not sure," I said unable to keep the emotion from my voice.

Cackling laughter erupted, filling the air with its harsh cords. "Blackwood thinks you murdered the witch! He is a disloyal puss-filled grub! Never trust a Blackwood," she hissed. "Thou art as fat as butter, thou murderous beggar! Thou art a boil! A plague sore, a sodden-witted-"

"I didn't murder her!"

"It is foretold!"

"I haven't murdered any witch."

"Are you not forgetting Millicent. You turned her into a goat and then she was burned to a crisp!"

"I didn't burn her to a crisp. The dragon did it."

"And he, my dear sodden-witted plague sore, is an extension of you!"

"Just shut up!"

"And do you know what else the ancient ones foretell?"

"No!" I said with nauseous roiling dropping like a deadweight in my stomach.

"They foretell that you will burn at the stake too! Burned to a crisp!"

A chill ran through my body.

"Liar!" I hissed. "You're just a poisonous and lying old goat!"

She cackled. "'Tis foretold," she cawed as I turned to run back to the cottage, "and Hetty will have her revenge on us all."

As I reached the front door, Garrett pulled into the driveway and I grabbed my coat and joined him relieved that he had stepped out to greet me. Wrapped in the comfort of his arms, nothing could harm me, at least for those perfect moments.

"Liv, are you alright?" he asked. "Stupid question, I know, but ... what in the name of Thor is going on?"

I told him about finding Priscilla tied to the burning tree and how the farmer had driven up just as I'd pulled the petrol cannister from the hedgerow. "The fire could have spread towards it. I thought it would make the situation worse ..."

"Not sure how it could get worse," he said. "You were seen at the scene with the petrol cannister in hand and the whole village knows that Priscilla had a vendetta against you."

"It's worse than that!"

"How?"

"I threatened to kill her the day before! She came to the cottage with a mob. They were threatening us. I lost my cool and when she grabbed me ... I don't know what happened, but my aunts said I screeched that I was going to kill her and then turned her into a goat!"

"So it can get worse," he said.

"Yes! They'll arrest me Garrett and throw away the key."

He shook his head.

"And ... and Lucifer and Old Mawde say I'm going to burn to a crisp just like Hetty Yikkar! It is foretold!" My voice reached a crescendo and then I began to sob.

Garrett crushed me to his chest. "There, there," he soothed. "No one is going to burn you to a crisp and the evidence against you is all circumstantial."

"Circumstantial? Like threatening to kill her and then being found with a petrol cannister in my hand whilst she's burning and tied to a tree."

"I know it looks bad but-"

"It is bad!"

"Let's stay calm, Liv. I know that you didn't do this. If you'd wanted to kill someone you wouldn't have burned her."

"Although ... although the sign above her said 'Witch' and that could be twisted round to be a distraction."

"Distraction?"

"Yes, so I put it there to lead people to think that someone who hates witches did it."

He nodded. "It could, Liv, but the sign didn't say 'Witch'."

"It didn't?"

"No, it said 'Bitch'."

"I'm confused. I'm sure it said 'Witch'."

"You read what you expected to see, I think. But it definitely said 'Bitch'. I've just come from the crime scene. From what I've heard of the woman, the title fits."

I sagged against him. "She wasn't very nice," I agreed.

"And there were other people she had upset. She had quite a reputation for financial misconduct."

"She did?"

He nodded. "She was under investigation for fraud, Liv."

"So ... so someone else could have done it?"

"That's right. So, stay calm. We'll get to the bottom of this." He stroked my hair and I soaked in his strength.

"Thank you," I said.

"That's what future husbands are for," he said.

I sighed remembering the petition for marriage.

"What is it?"

"Oh ... the petition ..."

"And don't worry about that either," he soothed. "Uncle Tobias is working on it."

"But your mother ... what if she doesn't like me?"

"She will! Yule's not far away now and you'll get your chance to impress her then."

I held back an inner groan. "If I'm not in prison!"

He laughed. "Stop worrying. Listen, I know things are fraught around here, so let's go out for the rest of the day. I'm away for the rest of the week and-"

"But what if the police want to arrest me?"

"They'll want to question you, but that can wait. Where shall we go? I think we both need to de-stress."

I remembered a café up on the moors with fabulous views. "We could go up to Moorside Café," I suggested.

"Good idea. Bit cold at this time of year, but they have a wood burner inside." He took my hand and led me to the car.

I stalled as I remembered the chaos in the village. "Can we pass by the shop and check that the windows aren't broken, please. I had to scrub graffiti off the other day and if tensions are higher ..."

"I know you don't want to hear this, Liv, but given the tensions in the village it may be better to give it a wide berth, especially with it being so close to the Night-"

"I wish they didn't call it the Night of Good Fires!" I blurted. "There's nothing good about burning us alive!" My emotion surfaced and I choked back a sob as the image of Priscilla roped to the smouldering tree, heat rising in white clouds, returned to my memory.

"Hetty will have her revenge on your saggy, puss-filled backside!" screeched Old Mawde, her head pushed through the gap in the fence.

"Ignore whatever she's saying, Liv. Come on, we'll drive past the shop and then go up to the café."

Chapter Twenty-Six

Thankfully, the road to the village didn't pass the site of Priscilla's death so the scorched tree was out of sight. Garrett took the back roads, and we entered the village by a narrow lane that led past Hrok's house. Ahead the road was blocked.

"What's going on?" I asked and peered into the distance.

Several cars were pulled onto the verge, including a police car. The lane was filled with people, several holding placards.

"They're hounding him again!" I said in exasperation.

Garrett pulled up behind the police car. Several police officers stood at the entrance gate. Hrok stood behind the iron gate, his face thunderous. Behind him, at the front door was Æstrid with Trixie held under her arm. The dog was yapping. One of the windows had broken panes.

Several men and women were clustered around the policemen.

"They murdered Priscilla!" a woman screeched as we stepped out of the car.

"They burned her alive!"

"Arrest them!" the woman screeched. "They're murderers!"

"Are they blaming Hrok for murdering Priscilla," I asked.

"It sounds like it."

"But that's crazy. Why would he kill Priscilla?"

"The petition ..."

Garrett stepped in between the heckling woman and the policemen then turned to face the crowd. He held a hand in the air and the noise grew quiet. "Now," he said. "If you could all take a step back away from the property, please." As instructed, the group moved back. Calm seemed to have descended. He turned back to the officers, spoke with them for several moments, then turned back to the crowd.

"Mrs. Dedman's murder has been a shock to us all. The entire village is grieving her loss, but we must not allow our emotions to lead us into rash, and criminal, actions. I can assure you that we are doing everything in our power to discover just who the murderer is."

"She did it!" a woman screeched from the crowd.

I turned to see a screwed-up face, filled with loathing, white teeth bared within a black and straggling beard.

The woman's shout was accompanied by shouts of agreement.

Garrett held up a silencing hand.

"There may be multiple suspects in this case, but I can assure you that we will investigate every avenue."

"What! When the murderer is your girlfriend?" a man called. "Not likely!"

The crowd erupted.

"She's a murderer."

"Carmichael did it!"

"They both did it!"

"They were seen dancing naked in the very field she was killed in three days ago."

"They were calling the devils to dance with them!"

"They sacrificed Priscilla for their black magic!"

Hrok moved along behind the iron railings until we were adjacent then he crooked a finger and beckoned me.

Ignoring the screech of "They're in it together!" I stepped up to the gate.

"They say I killed a woman!"

"They say I killed her too."

"Did you?"

"Of course not!"

"I have to be honest, Livitha, I am on the verge of taking things into my own hands."

This was serious. Casting magick against the villagers was a punishable crime.

"Don't do that. The last thing you need is the Witches' Institute charging you with Acts of Violence."

"Just a little calming spell ..."

I shook my head. "Casting spells against them is why they have the Night of Good Fires. Hetty-"

"Maybe Hetty was justified," he said with a glance to the mob. "They're almost hysterical!" As he spoke, his eyes focused on the crowd. I followed his gaze. Among the crowd, staring in our direction was Prudence Wellwisher. She appeared to watch Hrok for several more moments then turned away and walked towards the village.

Hrok remained silent as he watched her walk away.

"That's Prudence Wellwisher," I said. "Do you know her?"

"Prudence Wellwisher? That's not a real name!"

"I know! She moved into the village a few weeks ago."

"Did she, now."

"Yes. She runs a group, well, it's more like a cult, that promotes sexual continence and purity."

"Is that so," he said, and his lips set to a hard line.

"Priscilla, the woman who died, was one of her acolytes. She's the one who started the petition against you."

"A petition! Well, that's a new way of getting rid of us."

"Priscilla was trying to get the council to have you evicted. She started the petition, but I think Prudence was behind it all."

"Yes," he said, narrowing his eyes as he looked beyond my shoulder. "I bet she was."

"Do you know her?" I asked.

"No," he replied and then, without another word, turned and strode back to the house. As he disappeared inside, the door slammed behind him, and the dog's yap became muffled.

The situation in the village had become dire. The Night of Good Fires was approaching and the oppressive sense of doom that had hung over the cottage for the past few weeks had become overwhelming. Now it was present in the village like a dark and ominous cloud. Death was lurking in the shadows. An uncomfortable awareness that he would come knocking on my door was a feeling I couldn't shake. Hrok and the Slawston crones were in danger, as was every witch in the village. The villagers' animosity towards us was growing and the comments among the crowd made it clear that they were on the precipice of launching into a fear-driven witch hunt. It could already have begun.

I had my suspicions about who killed Priscilla, and my money was on Prudence. She was the one figure who stood out and had a link to the murdered woman through the cult she had instigated. She had brought her cultish club to the village and spread hate in the form of her 'purity club'. That hate had been directed at Hrok. My suspicion that she had done so deliberately because she knew who he was rather than just disapproved of his lifestyle had been confirmed by the looks they exchanged outside his house. He had recognised her, I felt sure. She had seen that recognition in his face and then turned away. There were secrets between them that I was determined to discover. I made a plan to put Prudence under surveillance and tomorrow I would visit the Council of Witches and ask them to confirm just who the familiar, Goubert, belonged to.

Despite the problems in the village, and my impending arrest, I found the trip to the moorside café enjoyable, and I even managed to put thoughts of Priscilla and Prudence to one side and just appreciate being with Garrett. He was going away tomorrow, and we both wanted to enjoy our time together. We visited a local market town and bought plum loaf from a baker and sausages from the butcher then walked along the river. The early winter sun was bright and surprisingly warm but, as clouds shifted to cover it, it grew cold and we decided to head back home. As we drew closer to Haligern, I grew concerned that a police car would be waiting along with a team ready to arrest me, but as we pulled into the driveway it was empty. Garrett pulled up close to the entrance.

"Liv," he glanced out of the car window towards the moon which was close to being full. "I hate to leave you when the tension in the village is so ... tense, but I can't miss this course. I'll be back in a week."

"After the full moon," I stated. *Of course.*

A frown creased his brow. "Yep."

"I'm going to visit the Council of Witches," I blurted, unable to keep the decision to myself. "My aunts told me not to go, but I have to."

"Why would your aunts tell you not to go?"

"The Council is well known for poking their nose in where it isn't wanted. They don't want their attention on us, I guess, but I have to find out who Prudence Wellwisher is, and her familiar's name is the only lead we've got."

"I see. That makes sense to me. They do keep records of every familiar and who it belongs to."

I was pleased that he knew and seemed to understand.

I reached for the car door.

"Hey!" he said. "You're forgetting something."

"What?" I asked.

"My kiss!" His smile broadened, lit by the moonlight shining into the car.

I leant forwards and our lips met. His were soft and warm. He slipped his arm across my back and crushed me to him. The intensity of his hold made me gasp—literally. "Ugh! You're suffocating me," I managed. His grip released and I took a lungful of air.

"Sorry!" he chuckled. "I don't know my own strength. It's just ..." He took hold of my chin and held my gaze. "I cannot wait to marry you, Livitha Erikson and make you Mrs. Blackwood."

The prickle of tears was instantly in my nose.

"Me too," I managed.

"I'd rather not be Mrs. Blackwood," he joked.

I batted his sleeve.

"Are you sure you're alright?" he asked.

"Sure, why wouldn't I be."

"Oh, I don't know. Perhaps being beaten up and then stumbling across a burning body and then being accused of murder could have upset you a bit, I guess." He smiled but I recognised the genuine concern in his eyes. "And then there's the bit about the village going on a witch hunt and wanting to burn you at the stake."

"Thanks for the reminder!"

"Liv, I would stay ... but it's not possible."

"I know," I said. "You've got another course to go on." I wanted to add that it was odd that the courses and his emergency calls always fell on a full moon but bit it back; that was a conversation for another day.

As Garrett left, and the car's taillights disappeared back down the driveway, my mood darkened. Inside were my aunts along with havoc-wreaking energies and fraught nerves. Renweard had taken to avoiding the kitchen whilst they were there, only slinking in beside the fire once they had gone to bed and Benny had been missing for a few days. Bess, the temperamental whippet had become a nuisance, and sat quivering against Aunt Beatrice's legs for much of the day. Home was no longer a refuge and for the first time in my life, the strain of being inside was greater than being outside.

My plan was to go in, pop my head around the kitchen door where I expected my aunts to be gathered drinking a cup of hot chocolate before bed, say goodnight and then go upstairs. This served two purposes. Firstly, I wouldn't get embroiled in one of their disagreements and secondly, I could keep my visit to the Witches' Council a secret. I was determined to find out Prudence Wellwisher's true identity and, as they kept a record of all familiars throughout the centuries, then they were my most promising lead. I knew my aunts would disapprove and try to dissuade me from going, or worse, forbid my visit.

As I took the steps to the cottage, I was surprised to find a number of travelling cases on the doorstep. Three besom brooms were also lined up against the wall.

"Visitors," I murmured and opened the door.

The hallway was quiet and when I peered around the corner of the kitchen door only Aunt Beatrice was there. More surprising was the hat on her head. She was also wearing a long winter coat. Buttoned from collar to her knees it tapered at the waist then flowed into a full skirt that skimmed the ankles of her travelling boots.

"Are you going somewhere?" I asked, unable to conceal my surprise.

"Ah, Livitha, you're back. We've been waiting for you."

Chatter from the drawing room grew distinct as the door was opened and then Aunts Thomasin and Euphemia appeared at the kitchen doorway. They too had their coats and hats on.

"There are cases on the doorstep and your brooms," I said. The times I had heard them mention going away until their existence was a distant memory surfaced, and my belly did a watery flip. They had said nothing concrete about going. Were they leaving me behind? "Are you going somewhere?" I asked as the words stuck in my throat.

"Oh, dear," said Aunt Beatrice. "We didn't mean to upset you!"

I looked from one aunt to the other. "Where are you going? Are you leaving me?"

"Goodness no!" said Aunt Thomasin.

"Well, we are, but not for long," soothed Aunt Euphemia. "We just need some time away. Things are becoming very strained around here."

"All the bickering has begun to drive poor Raif round the bend and he has insisted that he and Loveday take a holiday until after the Night of Good Fires has passed."

"Oh," I said. "So, it's just for a few days?"

Aunt Thomasin nodded. "It is."

"But I'm not invited?" I asked.

Each avoided eye contact with me.

"It's not that you're not invited. It was a quick decision," said Aunt Beatrice with a glance at the ceiling.

I followed her gaze. A scorch mark sat between two beams.

"Loveday nearly set fire to the place after Beatrice made mention of Hetty's lost grimoires and Raif lost his temper."

"That's when he said they were leaving."

"And you're going with them?"

"Oh, no, we're not going to be gooseberries. We thought we'd let them take some time away together, just the two of them."

"And where are you going?"

"We're going to stay with the Chidwick crones. They live on Grimsay island. It's in the Outer Hebrides so very remote—a perfect getaway from all of this tension."

"And Aunt Loveday?"

"She's going down to Cornwall. She and Raif are spending Yule with Betty and Emmanuell Seeze of Penzance."

"So, I'll be alone?"

"It's for the best, dear. Someone needs to stay and keep an eye on the shop-"

"And Old Mawde and Hegelina. We can't ask Mrs. Driscoll to milk the two old baggages!"

With Aunt Loveday and Uncle Raif already on their way to Cornwall, my aunts said goodbye and with their suitcases strapped to their brooms, ascended into the night sky like crows taking flight at midnight. Their forms quickly disappeared into the darkness, and I returned to an empty house. Lucifer looked up from the cushion beside the fire, gave me a cursory glance, then closed his eyes and went back to sleep.

Tired and now bereft, I made my way to bed. However, there was one upside to my abandonment, I would not have to lie about going to the Witches' Council tomorrow and what my aunts didn't know wouldn't hurt them.

Chapter Twenty-Seven

The following morning, I rose early, milked the taciturn goats, fed Lucifer, ate my breakfast, and set off for the Council of Witches.

With the Satnav set for Goxhill, the closest village to the Council's location, I set off. I took the road through the village that would lead me to the main roads and then the motorway, passing Hrok's house on the way through. All was quiet and there was no sign of protestors or more damage to the property. I also passed Hetty Quinelle's cottage. A light shone in an upstairs room. Whoever Prudence Wellwisher was, she was a night owl or scared of the dark.

The journey to Goxhill was uneventful, and I arrived in the lane, where the Council of Witches was hidden, as dark was giving way to a thin, grey light. It was too early to knock on the door, and I felt it improper to drive up to the hut until the sun had risen. My stomach gurgled. With the engine switched off, the temperature in the car soon dropped but I didn't want to turn it back on. It was a waste of fuel and was noisy. I lit a witch light and let it hover in the passenger seat and focused my thoughts on warmth and soft glowing light.

Brighten! "Gebierhtest!" I commanded.

The witch light intensified, spreading out its yellow glow to illuminate the steering wheel.

Be hot! "Geweallan!"

To my surprise, the light began to throb. It threw out an orange light and began to exude warmth. Pleased with myself, I reached into my bag and pulled out my sandwiches. Hot air circulated around the car, and I took a bite. After the second bite, the heat was becoming a little stuffy and had a hard edge to it. The light was a brighter orange. It pulsed and intense heat radiated outwards. A blast of hot air hit my cheek and fingers as I held the sandwich to my mouth. The light sparked. Seconds later it began to crackle. The heat was becoming unbearable at a rapid rate. An odour of singeing fabric and melting plastic seeped through the car. I had to turn it down!

"Lessen!" I said. "Stop!"

The orange light flickered but did not dim and the heat remained intense.

Cold! "Cealda!" I commanded. The heat remained. *Stop!* "Geswīc!" I shouted with my hand on the door handle.

The light switched off.

"Thank Thor!" I exclaimed.

A hard rap at the window startled me and I dropped my sandwich. Tuna, mayonnaise, and lettuce spread across my lap.

I turned to see a woman's face staring at me. Her face was drawn into a hard scowl. Bessie Yikkar. I rolled down the window. She took a step back and wafted her hand in front of her face.

"What a horribly hot and fishy smell!" she said.

"Tuna!" I said holding up the sloppy remnants of sandwich.

She pulled open the door.

"Step out of the vehicle, Livitha Erikson, and explain your presence."

As she caught my eyes in a hard stare, it crossed my mind that perhaps I had made a mistake. There was also the issue of her last name. I placed the remnants of sandwich back in their wrap of waxed paper and left the car.

"Lock it," she instructed. "We will walk to the hut. I presume you are here to visit."

I locked the car as instructed, answered yes, then followed her as she walked ahead. Her stride was long, and I had to increase my pace to keep up. She remained silent until we came to the narrow break in the hedgerow. I remembered being forced to put my foot down on the accelerator and drive the car through on my first visit. I'd gripped the steering wheel and hunched my shoulders, sure that the car would become wedged between the gap. It had opened wide enough to let the car through before closing behind us. This time we walked through. The movement of the trees was disorientating. The trunks creaked in protest and the leaves rustled above me. They seemed angry and I wondered if it was me they objected to.

"Do they do that every time?" I asked.

"Move? Of course they do."

"I meant make that noise. It's as if they're struggling."

"Well of course they are. Their roots lie deep within the ground. They are less than happy at being forced to move – lazy creatures! – they complain every time."

I considered the trees from a different perspective and as I cast a glance at the trunk was sure I discerned the face of an old man among the bark. The lips seemed to pucker and contort as it moved back into place, like a fat old man struggling to do up the button on his trousers the morning after a large meal.

After walking through the hedgerow, we were greeted by the Council's hut.

Beyond was an area of overgrown scrubland. At its centre sat a derelict Nissen hut, the curve of its corrugated roof overhung with trees. A grime-smeared window sat to the side of a narrow door with a rotting, now slanted, door frame.

As before, it appeared to be derelict.

"Do you remember the words you must say upon entering? And those you must say upon leaving?"

"I do," I said, the memory of standing before the derelict hut on my last visit surprisingly clear in my memory.

"Good, now remember, you must pronounce them properly or you will get trapped."

"My aunts said the magic was very mischievous and loves to cause trouble."

"It is so. Now, to be sure, repeat after me."

She recited the words, slowly and with full enunciation. Then began to step towards the derelict hut. For a moment I thought that it hadn't worked. "Come along, Livitha. Recite."

I recited the words.

The air in front of the Nissen hut shimmered and the façade of decay fell away. The hut remained but was now in pristine condition. The brickwork front looked freshly built, the door was shiny with black gloss paint, and beneath the window a manger-style basket filled with ivy and bright yellow winter aconites hung. A single car was parked to the side and smoke rose in a twist from the chimney in its curved roof. The tree that had been heavy with ripe apples on my last visit was bare.

Bessie opened the door and beckoned me to follow. "Come along in. It's only Effie and me here at the moment."

The interior was as I had remembered it. At least twenty feet wide and nearly forty feet long, the first ten feet or so were given over to a reception area laid with well-worn oak floorboards. Either side, floor-to-ceiling shelves were packed with books, many of them leather bound and ancient, others were modern paperbacks or hardback covers. A waist-height and gated partition sat across the width of the hut, behind it were several desks, each piled with books. Beyond the desks were two emerald-green velvet sofas. This area was lit by lamplight and between them was a coffee table, again piled with books and a single coffee mug.

Halfway along one side, a stone-built fireplace, that would have looked more at home in a primitive country home, dominated. This section of the room was filled with open shelves stocked with jars and potion bottles and hung with drying herbs. There were also two huge and ancient pantry-like lockable cupboards each with a large iron key in their keyholes. A cauldron hung from an iron hook within the chimney. On my last visit, Anne Whittle had been working at the cauldron and claimed that she had known we were going to pay a visit.

As Bessie led me further into the room Effie emerged from one of the large cupboards along the hut's wall. She was on the plump side but curvaceous with dark, glossy hair worn in a messy chignon. Tight jeans accentuated a full but curvaceous figure.

"Oh!" she said, looking up from the large book she held open in her hands.

"Livitha Erikson," stated Bessie, "of the Haligern coven. She is here to visit for unnamed reasons."

"Of course! We met on your last visit." Effie offered a broad smile above the glasses perched on her nose. "You've travelled miles then," she said. "Can I get you a cup of tea?"

I remembered the warmth with which she'd greeted me last time and I determined to get to know her better. I'd liked her immediately and it would be refreshing to have a friend I could talk to without being guarded over every word I uttered.

"Yes, thanks," I replied.

She tacked across the floor in her high heels, so much more glamorous than me in my mum jeans, walking boots, and fuchsia fleece.

"Effie is a direct descendant of Frioðulf, king of Lindsey," Bessie said, "and she's training as a Vardlokkur."

Bessie had made the same brag during my previous visit. "That's very impressive," I said and was rewarded by a broad smile.

"After all this time, it is a marvel. And she is taking to instruction very well. Of course, she has only just started her apprenticeship, just as you have started your novitiate. How are you finding it? Are your aunts teaching you well?"

I thought back to the months of haphazard instruction. "Yes, very well. Aunt Loveday is very happy with my progress."

"And you have begun your own grimoire?"

I nodded. "I have."

"Excellent."

We chatted for several more minutes as Bessie made polite conversation, asking about the health of my aunts. Once Effie returned with the tea and I had taken the first sip, her demeanour changed. "So, Livitha, I can be candid. It is unusual in the extreme for novices to turn up to the Council unannounced."

"I'm sorry! I didn't realise I needed an appointment. When we came before, I don't recall my aunts calling ahead."

"Correct, they didn't. They came as a matter of urgency. Protocol and etiquette were put aside. So, please inform us, of exactly why you are here."

I decided to be forthright. "I need to find out to whom a familiar by the name of Goubert belongs."

She raised a brow. "For what purpose?"

"There's a newcomer in the village. She calls herself Prudence Wellwisher, but I'm sure that is a fake name. My aunts know of no one by that name. And Lucifer tells me that she has a familiar named Goubert."

"And this woman has not revealed herself to you as a witch?"

"No. She is causing trouble in the village though. She seems to be forming a cult and promoting it to the village housewives."

"That is cause for concern."

I relaxed. I had been right to visit. "I was hoping that you held records about familiars and their mistresses."

She nodded. "We do."

"So, could we take a look ... please?"

"Effemia, could you fetch the Record of Familiars, please?"

"Certainly," Effie replied and made her way to the largest of the cupboards.

I expected her to open the door and pull out a large volume but instead she walked inside as though it were the wardrobe leading to Narnia. I took a step towards the wardrobe, hoping to get a peek inside.

"Ahem!"

I stalled, realising I was committing a faux pas of unspoken etiquette and took a step back.

After several uncomfortable moments, Effie reappeared, a large and dusty tome held in outstretched arms. The book was massive, leatherbound, and ancient. She placed it on the closest desk with a thud. Whorls of dust eddied as it landed.

Bessie waved at the clouds. "Oh, dear, it is rather dusty," she said. "Fetch a cloth, dear. We shall wipe it down before opening it. Grubby thing!"

After wiping down the front of the book and the desk with a damp cloth and drying both, the tome was opened. The frontispiece showed an illustration of several creatures, including cats, dogs, rabbits, and crows surrounding a couple. The man held a staff and a large magpie sat on his shoulder whilst the woman, in full skirts and the traditional witch's pointed hat, held a besom broom. A black cat sat at her feet. The title page read, 'Recorde off Familyars from the Begyning'. Bessie began to turn over the pages, scanning the lines of text, each one the name of a familiar, to whom they belonged, and the date they were first known to be paired. "Obviously, this is a copy of an older book. We have done our best to collect and record all familiars and their owners but obviously much of that knowledge is lost to time. Occasionally we can fill in some missing information when we come across one of our own with that knowledge."

The history of our people was fascinating and I could have spent hours listening to Bessie's recollections, but I had only one mission today and that was to discover just who Prudence Wellwisher really was.

"Goubert you say the familiar's name is ..."

"Yes. We think it's an Anglo-Norman name, at least that's what my aunts remember."

"It does sound as though it could be. We could be here for some time," she said with a sigh then began to run her finger down a list of entries with earnest before turning over the huge page. After several minutes she muttered beneath her breath and then stopped with her finger hovering over a name. "Hah! I have one. Goubert, a marmalade tomcat belonging to Sybil de Normandie. Could that be your troublesome crone?" She looked at me for confirmation.

"I'm not sure," I replied. "I don't know what the familiar looks like."

She raised a brow. "It would help if you did!" Returning her gaze to the book, she continued her search.

Several minutes passed. "Here's another. Goubert, a black tomcat with a white paw, front and left, belonging to Hester Janikin of the Wharram Percy Janikins. They were paired in 1087 so that would fit your Anglo-Norman hypothesis."

"Isn't Wharram Percy a deserted medieval village?" I asked.

"It is. Hester was one of the reasons it became deserted."

"So, she has a record of harm?"

"Well, I wouldn't say that. She took in a traveller who turned out to have an infestation of fleas. The fleas were carriers of the plague. I'm afraid, poor Hester managed to depopulate the village without casting a single hex. However, being the only one to live through the plague in the village, she was forced to leave and seek a living elsewhere. If memory serves, I do believe she married quite soon after."

"Do you know who to?"

"I shall check. Effemia, please bring me the book of Marriages."

Effie disappeared into the largest cupboard and re-emerged minutes later carrying another huge and leatherbound book. She sat it on the table with a thud and whorl of dust. The procedure of cleaning then name searching was repeated, but this time the focus was on the sixteenth century. "Aha! I have found her. She married Hrok son of Halvard in 1538. He was a sorcerer. A good match, I would say."

"Hrok, son of Halvard," I repeated managing to keep my shock hidden.

The connection was confirmed! Prudence Wellwisher was in fact Hester Janikin, ex-wife of the sorcerer, Hrok son of Halvard! It all made sense. A vindictive ex-wife determined to cause havoc for whatever grievances she had against her ex-husband. By focusing the villagers' ire on Hrok and the sisters, she was causing him immense grief.

Hell hath no fury like a woman scorned!
But why make the women hairy?
So that he found them unappealing.
She's jealous! She still loves him!

"That's interesting," I managed.

"So, do you think that either of these women is your witch?"

"It's very possible, although which one, I am not sure."

"There is one way to find out."

"Oh?"

"Ask," said Bessie and closed the book. "The familiar will tell you."

"Lucifer tried. He would only name her as Prudence."

"Loyal," said Bessie with satisfaction. "That is good to know."

"But not helpful."

"No, but if you are clever enough you could trick the familiar into telling you the truth."

Chapter Twenty-Eight

It was late afternoon when I arrived back in the village, and with the cottage now empty, I headed to the shop. I noticed a customer peering in through the window with a twinge of guilt; achieving consistent opening hours had been an issue since we had launched, and I had worked hard over the past weeks to open on time. The wall to the side of the window had been defaced again, and 'Burn the witch!' was written in bright pink and chalky capitals. This told me two things a) Priscilla was definitely not the culprit, and b) the villagers' animosity towards us had not dwindled.

The customer walked away, and I resisted shouting to tell them that the shop was open; I needed some time to unwind after the journey and this morning's bombshell reveal that Prudence Wellwisher aka Hester Janikin was Hrok's ex-wife. On the journey home, I had become convinced that it was she who had cast a hex on the village housewives in order to punish them for talking to Hrok whilst simultaneously making them repulsive to him. The women I had seen Hrok talk to, were the ones who had become hairy.

I also deduced that whilst it was Hrok who had punished the abusive husband by casting a spell to make him walk straight into a lamppost, it had been Prudence/Hester who had caused the woman to trip into the road and flicked her skirt above her waist.

It all made sense—Hester was still in love with her husband and was jealous of his relationship with the Slawston sisters and the potential love interests in the village – hence the vendetta against Hrok and the plague of hairiness afflicting the village housewives.

"She's a true bunny boiler," I said as I let myself into the shop. "A proper nutjob!"

I planned to confront her with my evidence that afternoon, but first I was desperate for a cup of tea and a bit of downtime after the long drive home. With the sign flipped to 'open' and the hope that no one would enter for at least ten minutes, I made my way to the kitchen and put on the kettle. There was a chill to the shop too, so I placed kindling and logs in the burner and lit it whilst the tea brewed.

I had only just taken my first sip of tea when the bell tinkled, and the shop door opened. With an inward sigh, I made my way to the front to be greeted by an unfamiliar man. He scanned the shop then beamed my way.

"Can I help you?" I asked.

He passed a chubby hand through dark and greasy hair. "I hope so," he replied.

Something about the way he spoke then peered at me through thick-rimmed glasses – the scanning of my body from chest downwards – reminded me of the lecherous shifter, Cyril Talbot. The man was of a similar build, on the short side, rotund and with shoulders rounded by fat. His hair flopped over his glasses and, as he pushed it back up, I noticed the overly long and dirty fingernails. A waft of body odour rose to greet me as I stepped behind the counter. Despite my revulsion, I smiled. "Is there anything in particular I can help you with?" I asked, hoping his reply wouldn't be laced with inuendo.

"I'm looking for a woman!" he said.

His reply was far worse than I had expected. "I'm sorry but we don't ... sell women."

He chuckled. "Glad to hear it. That would be sex trafficking," he said.

I grimaced. "Human trafficking," I corrected. "Or slavery."

He gave another throaty chuckle.

"We sell creams and lotions." I gestured to the shelves, now relieved that the nether-region cream was still in production and not for sale, "for dry skin, and pimples, that kind of thing."

"I phrased it wrong," he said. "I'm looking for a gift for a woman."

I groaned at my stupidity. "I'm so sorry! I thought you meant ..."

He waved a hand. "Not to worry, but the truth is that I was hoping that you could help me find a woman too."

I didn't want to stumble into more incorrect presumptions. "Find a woman?"

"Yes. I know she lives around here because I've seen one of your bags behind her."

"I'm sorry, I'm not following."

"The bag. It said 'Haligern Apothecary' on it. It was behind her in the video. That's how I know she lives around here."

"I see," I said wondering if I should call the police to inform them of a potential stalker.

"I'll show you!" He pulled out his mobile and began tapping on the screen.

Seconds later he thrust it in my face. It showed a bearded and hairy woman in a suggestive pose.

He growled as he glanced at the screen. I glanced towards the door - an escape route should I need it - and began to wonder if he was a Talbot and then if the woman on the screen was a Talbot.

"Is she ... your girlfriend?" I asked.

"I wish!" he replied. "She's sexy, isn't she."

I nodded and made a noncommittal noise. "And you want to buy a gift for her?"

"I do, but first I need to know where she lives."

Ask him to leave. Close the shop! "Oh."

"She's a sexy beast!" the man said. "A true hairy housewife. I have to find her. She's the real deal; a proper bearded lady, not one of the fake ones. You can tell because the hairs go all the way-"

"I'm sorry!" I blurted. "But I don't know her or where she lives."

"You wouldn't believe how many of the women lie just to get money. No, Mandy is the real deal. I bet you could give those curls a tug and they wouldn't come off."

Hysteria began to rise but I choked it back. "Mandy?" I squeaked.

"Do you know her?" he asked, his hopes rising.

"Can I see the photo again?"

He held up the screen. I squinted for better focus. Hysteria bubbled. The woman pictured had a red and curling beard and matching chest hair. The image scrolled to another one, this time the face was clear. It was Mandy Braithwaite.

"Did she send you these photos?" I asked, desperate to keep my voice under control.

He shook his head. "No. They're from a website, "Furries Only". She's in the specialist section, 'Real & Furry Housewives'. It's a niche thing."

"I can tell," I said as another image of Mandy rolled into view. "I think that one is a little too much for me." I cast my glance aside. Seeing Mandy's splayed nether regions was more than I could stomach. My mind felt singed.

"I've promised to help her."

"Oh?" I said with more than a little curiosity.

"Yeah. I'm going to prove to the haters that her beard is real."

"I see."

"So, do you recognise her?"

I shook my head.

"But she has a Haligern Apothecary bag behind her. See!" He stabbed at the screen.

"We sell a lot of our products as gifts," I said. "Orders come in from all over the country as well as abroad. She could even be in a different country."

His shoulders sagged. "You mean she doesn't live here."

"I don't think so," I lied.

He breathed a great sigh. I could almost see the cloud of sour breath. *Please leave!* "I'm sorry I couldn't be of any help."

His brow furrowed.

The clock struck five. "And I'm very sorry, but we're about to close. I think the café stays open until six if you need refreshments." I managed a smile, relieved when he took the hint and walked out of the shop. With the man gone, I grabbed a cleansing wand, lit it, and walked around the shop, wafting the burning herbs to rid the place of his lingering smell and grubby energy.

Relieved that the ordeal was over, I locked the shop and made my way to Hetty Quinelle's cottage where I intended to confront Prudence Wellwisher aka Hester Janikin and ask her to leave the village before any more damage could be done.

Chapter Twenty-Nine

The cottage stood in grounds with a lawn at the front and to the sides with a pathway leading to the door. A picturesque wooden archway with a gate was flanked either side by a waist-height hedge. Inside, Prudence Wellwisher, seen through open curtains, moved between the rooms. From the little I knew of her, I presumed that she was a powerful witch and the evidence that she dabbled in the darker side of magick was perhaps evident in her taking Hetty Quinelle's cottage. I had determined to confront her, but with each passing minute my courage was beginning to fail. I was a novitiate about to confront a possibly dark and dangerous witch without the back up of my aunts.

You defeated Millicent.

I did.

Without your aunts.

That's true, but I had the dragon ...

"Eep!" Something slithered around my ankles.

"What on earth was that?" Lucifer said with a disparaging voice as he stepped across my shoe.

"Lucifer!" I said, my heart now beating hard against my chest. "You scared me."

"Well, you make stupid noises when you're scared and anyway, you need to be alert for danger, Mistress. It has been foretold that you will burn to a crisp at the stake. I would rather that did not happen."

I listened to his words with rising horror. "I will not be burning to a crisp any time soon!" I retorted, refusing to listen to his doom-laden prophecy. It couldn't be true. "Witches are not burned at the stake anymore!"

"They burned Priscilla."

"She was not a witch, and she was tied to a tree."

"Same thing," he said. "Now, if you would be so kind as to confront the witch in yonder cottage, I would appreciate it. I have been sorely neglected since your aunts left. There has been no one to pour milk, port, or even water into my saucer! I am dying of thirst and the punishment for such cruel treatment of a familiar is-"

"Lucifer, hush!" I said as Priscilla aka Hetty stepped to the window.

"She has not heard us. She is drawing the curtains to stop nosey snoopers such as yourself from seeing inside. Now, as I was saying, the punishment for maltreatment of familiars is really rather cruel. You see what they do is first shackle you to a chair and then begin to pluck-"

"And do you know what the punishment for the emotional abuse and terrorising of your Mistress is?"

Lucifer huffed. "No! But I'm quite sure you'll delight in telling me."

"I shall delight in it because you are being unnaturally cruel to me. Anyone would think that you wanted to see me burned to a crisp at the stake!" I hissed whilst keeping an eye on the cottage.

"Well ... it would be entertaining."

I shook my head. "You're just enjoying tormenting me. If you don't stop, I shall not be buying any more port and putting you on a diet of tinned cat food—the cheap stuff!" I threatened.

Lucifer hissed.

"Good, I'm glad that you understand-"

"I am not hissing at you, fool! Goubert is in the garden. He is bound to inform his mistress of our presence."

I took a step back.

Lucifer hissed as I stumbled, caught against an obstruction that had not been there only seconds before, and I turned to stare straight into the scowling face of Prudence Wellwisher.

"Prudence!" I blurted. "How nice to see you."

She grabbed my arm, and I felt her fingers like a steel and overpowering grip around my bicep as she forced me forward. Powerless, I was walked through the gate and then into the cottage. Once inside, she released her grip. My bicep throbbed as though it had been squeezed by a particularly zealous nurse taking my blood pressure.

We stood in the living room, surrounded by Hetty Quinelle's belongings. The old crone had had a dark sense of humour and stuffed bats hung from the ceiling as though in flight. I noticed a badly stuffed cat, hackles raised, one eye on me, the other on the ceiling, standing within a glass case on the sideboard wedged into the alcove beside the chimney breast. It had the characteristic comic horror of one of Marye of Pendlewick's unique taxidermy efforts. Lucifer hissed beside my ankle as he noticed the grotesquely stuffed cat.

"One of Hetty's familiars," Prudence said with spite and a glower to Lucifer. "Another one that did not know its place."

Lucifer slunk behind my legs.

"Leave him alone," I said.

Prudence turned her scowl on me. "Pray tell, Livitha, daughter of Soren, why you are snooping outside my home."

I felt my tongue thicken.

"And tell the truth, or I shall make your tongue swell until it doth choke you to death!"

My tongue began to feel a little bigger.

"Quick!" she said. "Before it is the size of a cucumber!" Her cackle was malicious.

My tongue doubled in size. "I want you to leave the village!" I blurted. My tongue instantly shrank, and I gagged.

"Whyever would I do that?" she asked. "I like it here. The women are ... fascinating."

"It was you who hexed them!" I said. "You made them hairy."

She watched me with a defiant glint in her eye.

"And I know why you did it! And I know who you really are!"

A twitch at the side of her mouth was the only evidence of a reaction.

"I doubt that," she said.

"You did it because you're Hester Janikin of Wharram Percy and you are Hrok, son of Halvard's ex-wife!"

Her lips thinned as I continued.

"You made the women hairy because you're so jealous of any woman who shows the slightest interest in Hrok. And you began a vendetta against the Slawston crones to force Hrok to give them up."

Hester began a slow and sardonic clap. "Very well done, Livitha daughter of Soren Erikson. However, there is one thing that you got wrong."

Everything I had said was either fact or based on sound conjecture. "What?" I asked.

"Hrok and I are still married. I am his wife, not his ex-wife."

"I see. Well, it makes no difference. Married or not, you are attacking the women because you still love him and want him back!"

Her brows rose in surprise, but she did not deny my appraisal of her motives. I went in for the kill. "And I also believe that it was you who killed Priscilla by tying her to a tree and burning her alive."

Hester shuddered and shook her head. "What a terrible accusation to make to a witch, Daughter of Soren. Very rude."

"I'm sorry, but I believe that you did it. The evidence is circumstantial but-"

"Why on earth would I kill Priscilla?" she asked, hands now on hips and her eyes locked to mine. "Although I don't blame whoever did it. She was a spiteful woman full of malice, particularly towards our kind." Her eyes narrowed. "I think this is just an effort at deflection. I had heard that it was *you* who had killed her. You certainly had motive."

"It was not me!"

"And it was not me."

"Prove it!"

"You prove it!" she countered.

"I was at home that evening," I said.

"Yes, but you found her whilst the tree was still burning and you were caught with a petrol cannister in your hand. She was killed in the earliest part of the morning when you were travelling to the village," she said with a triumphant smile.

"I would never burn a woman alive ... or a man ... or any creature!"

"Nor I," she retaliated. "And I have a far better alibi than you do."

"Tell me!" I demanded.

"I was with my husband—all night long," she said with a gloating and triumphant smile.

Shocked, I could find no words in rebuttal.

"Close your jaw, Livitha. It's not becoming of a lady to stand there with her mouth open."

"You were with Hrok? All night?"

"What is wrong? Do I not speak your language? Yes, I was with my husband."

"What about the Slawston sisters?"

She pulled a disgusted sneer. "Those women are yesterday's trash. Hrok has seen the error of his ways. He will be leaving the village with me, his one and only rightful wife."

"Oh," I managed. "And can he corroborate your alibi."

She gave a sneering laugh. "It is a night he will not forget!" she said. "The thing with being married for such a long time, Livitha, is that sometimes one must rein one's husband in. I'm sure you'll come to realise the truth of that. You are to marry a Blackwood, after all." She threw me a pitying smile. "But what Blackwood sees in you, I am becoming increasingly unsure of. It's not your wit or intellect, that is for certain."

"You're not a very nice person," I countered.

She stiffened and her lips thinned. "And you are fat."

"I want you to leave Haligern!"

"I shall leave when I want," she retorted.

"You will leave tonight, or I shall inform the Council of Witches that you have committed an Act of Violence Against Villagers. They are already aware of your presence here."

Her eyes widened. I had hit a nerve.

I pushed my advantage. "As you know, an Act of Violence Against Villagers is a punishable offence. It is the crime that Hetty Yikkar was accused of and what led to her fiery death here in this very village, the one that they are celebrating tomorrow night by burning her effigy at the stake."

Hester blanched.

"And I will enable your capture, just as my aunts enabled Hetty's, if you do not leave this village tonight!"

She swallowed.

"Did you know that Hetty Yikkar was posthumously exiled from our community? I'm quite certain that the Council would pass the same sentence upon you, dead or alive."

Her lips thinned. "Very well, Livitha. I see that you have inherited your father's spirit. My time here is over anyway. I have achieved what I set out to achieve. Hrok has pledged his heart to me and will be leaving with me."

"Did I hear my name mentioned?" Hrok stood in the doorway.

Hester walked to his side. "She's accusing me of murdering that dreadful woman! The one who was so vile towards you," she said with a pout.

Hrok's arm was instantly around her shoulders, his eyes suddenly cold as they met mine. "Hester has done no such thing. We were together the night Priscilla was killed."

Priscilla gave me a sly told-you-so glance from beneath her lashes.

"It was the morning, actually," I said, watching them both. Was Hrok telling the truth or was he covering for Hester? My thoughts whirled. After being hounded and vilified by Priscilla, Hrok certainly had motive, but it had been Hester/Prudence who had lit the fire of hate towards him. Uncle Tobias had known Hrok the longest and he hadn't said a bad word against him other than to scoff that there was 'no fool like an old fool' when he had heard of his living arrangements with the Slawston crones. My dealings with Hrok had shown him to be an honest and decent man. He had helped defeat Millicent and had only been kind and loving towards the Slawstons, as far as I knew. I didn't trust Hester, but I did trust Hrok.

"Okay, I accept that Hester didn't kill Priscilla, but she is responsible for the infestation of hairiness among the housewives."

"Don't be cross with me!" she simpered whilst gazing up at him. "I just couldn't stand the thought of them trying to flirt with you."

He sighed and shook his head. As he took her chin between his fingers and looked into her eyes, I wondered if Hester had cast a spell upon him.

"You always do have the best of intentions, my love." He turned his attention to me. "You must forgive her, Livitha, she only ever tries to help people, but unfortunately it often goes wrong. She's something of a jinx in that respect."

I resisted the urge to mention that she had caused enormous distress and havoc in the village, or that I knew she had been responsible for wiping out the entire population of

Wharram Percy. As I watched in wonder as he kissed her with enthusiasm, I simultaneously realised that Uncle Tobias had been right about Hrok's soft spot for women and that Priscilla's killer was still at large.

After leaving Hrok and Hester in an embrace of new-found passion, I returned to the shop. No fire would be lit in the hearth at the cottage, and I had no desire to return to a cold and empty home.

The warmth from the log burner helped ease my fraught nerves and as I fed the fairies a bowl of cheese mashed with a calmative elixir to help ease their excitement, the bell above the door tinkled. It was late, and the night was dark, and I swivelled round to see the man who had been looking for Mandy in the doorway.

I stood too quickly, and my voice was strained as I said, "We're closed."

The greasy-haired man pulled his foot back and stood in the doorway as though barred from entry.

"Sorry!" I said in a pleading manner.

"I ..."

I wanted to ask if he had found Mandy but didn't want to engage him in conversation. "We open again at ten in the morning," I said.

"It's just that I noticed that there's a lot of hairy women in this village. I thought you might know why. Is it a genetic thing?" he asked.

There was something deeply unpleasant about the man and my instinct was to get rid of him. I scoured my mind for something suitably off-putting and had a eureka moment.

"No," I said. "There's a convention on in the next town for women with PCOS," I lied.

"PCOS?"

"Yes. Polycystic ovary syndrome."

"Ovaries?" A flicker of uncertainty passed across his face. "Isn't that to do with women's bits?"

Bullseye! I recognised the reaction. Pascal had an aversion to anything remotely related to women's bodily functions and even Garrett paled if women's reproductive issues were mentioned. "Yes. Their hairiness is caused by *women's problems*," I hissed. "Just like Mandy's." I said this in conspiratorial tones.

He paled. "Women's problems," he repeated, his eyes glazing as he stared across my shoulder.

"Yes, like periods and things."

"And things," he murmured. A bead of sweat had appeared at his hairline. He swallowed.

"Yes, things like the menopause. That's when a woman's period-"

"Right. I see. So-"

"I know a lot about menstrual cycles and the menopause, ovarian dysfunction, things like that. Would you like to know more?"

He shook his head and began to step away, a flicker of fear in his eyes. I went in for the kill. "It's all perfectly natural," I said a little louder. "When a woman menstruates, it's her body's way of sloughing-"

The bell tinkled and then the door slammed behind him. I couldn't help a snort of laughter. The buzz of wings increased and then chittering snickers joined my giggles as the fairies swooped across the shop. They buzzed to the window, watching as the man walked with a quick pace across the road.

Tired after my day of travelling and sleuthing, and still in shock at Hrok's revelations, I made a hesitant journey home to a cold and empty cottage. Dreading tomorrow and the villager's gluttonous delight in burning the effigy of Hetty Yikkar, I went to bed, pulling the covers over my ears, and went to sleep.

Chapter Thirty

I woke with a start on the morning of the Night of Good Fires with one word repeating in my mind. Bitch.

I had assumed that the single word scrawled in pink chalk on the plaque above Priscilla's burning head had been the word 'Witch'. I had been wrong, reading what I expected to read.

"Bitch," I said and threw the duvet aside and swung my legs out of bed. Ignoring the ache my back and hips, I went straight to the bathroom to shower.

"Bitch," I repeated to my reflection in the mirror as I brushed my teeth. "Someone really hated you, Priscilla," I said as I replaced the toothbrush in its holder then waited for the acerbic comment from Lucifer. When it didn't come, I checked the room and realised that he hadn't woken me by digging his needle-like claws into my belly nor had he slept in my room last night.

Priscilla had been under investigation for fraud, but had it been enough to push someone to murder? I ran the details of her crime through my mind. She had befriended a man online and conned him out of his life savings by claiming that she needed money for a life-saving operation. The man, a widowed pensioner living on the Costa del Sol, believed they were in love and had given her more than ten thousand pounds for the imaginary surgery. Despite the offences committed against him, he seemed like an unlikely culprit.

"He lives in Spain and he's old and he reported the crime to the police. It wasn't him," I decided.

I checked the room for Lucifer. Usually, my efforts at solving a mystery were ridiculed by the acerbic cat. This time there was no sign of him.

"Where are you, Lou?" I whispered. "I could do with your help right now."

Without input from Lucifer, I pushed my thoughts forward as I dressed.

She was tied to a tree.

She wouldn't have let someone tie her to a tree.

Unless she liked being tied to a tree!

I shook the thought away.

Someone, or maybe more than one person, tied her to a tree.

Was she conscious when she was tied to the tree?

Had she been drugged?

Still no sign of Lucifer.

"I guess I'm on my own then," I huffed. "So," I said aloud, hoping that speaking would help clarify my thoughts, "she was forcibly tied to a tree after been driven up to the field ... if she were drugged it would be easier to get her in the car and tie her to the tree ... if it were just one person ..."

My thoughts were incohesive.

The tree ... bitch ...

A moment of clarity struck. "It was personal! Whoever tied her to the tree hated her and ... if she were drugged it would be easier to get her to co-operate."

My memory flitted through the past few weeks. Mandy had called Priscilla a bitch twice that I knew of. She had referred to her as a bitch whilst showing me the screenshot of Priscilla's beard *and* called her a bitch during their fight in the road.

"And she works in the pharmacy! She would know how to drug her up to make her pliable! Plus! ..." I grew excited as my thoughts cleared. "Mandy was making money on the Only Furries site. Priscilla would have ... Wait!" The memory of the catfight outside the shop replayed in my mind. 'And ... men love me even with my beard,' Mandy had shouted. 'You're just jealous because I've got more fans that you!' Priscilla had reacted as though scalded and dragged Mandy to the driver's seat and forced her into the car. She had driven away without another word and with a face so hard it would have turned Medusa to stone.

"Mandy had more fans than Priscilla!" I blurted. "Priscilla had an Only Furries page!" Stunned by the revelation, I stood with one arm thrust through my fleece and stared at the wall.

With my mind whirring, I returned from the stupor, zipped up the fleece, and made my way downstairs. The fire was unlit, the room cold, and there was no sign of Lucifer. Too churned up with thoughts of Mandy, Priscilla, and the Only Furries fan who had visited the shop, I decided to forego breakfast at home and grab a cup of tea and bacon butty at the café later. My objective now was to talk to Mandy and ask her some searching questions. Above all, I wanted to know if Priscilla, Queen of Purity, had an Only Furries page? If she did, then she was a rank hypocrite along with being a fraudster. If she did, it could also be a clue to her murder.

"You really weren't a very nice person, Priscilla," I muttered as I made my way to the car.

Mandy was at home and answered my knock at her door in her dressing gown, slightly out of breath, and with a flush on her cheeks, her coppery beard glossy and glinting in the morning sun. She opened the door with a smile that quickly disappeared as our eyes met.

It took a moment for me to speak; I had hoped that Hester's curse would be broken. "Mandy," I said. "I'm sorry for disturbing you-"

"Disturbing me?" she asked in a defensive tone. "What do you mean?"

"I ... just that I'm sorry to interrupt-"

"You haven't interrupted anything," she said.

"Right," I said. That she was lying was obvious and I was instantly suspicious that she was hiding something. "If you don't mind, I'd like to talk to you about a visitor I had to the shop?"

Her frown deepened.

"What visitor?"

"Can I come in and talk? It's a delicate matter," I said.

She glanced either side of the street, then took a step back to let me in, and ushered me into the kitchen.

"Take a seat," she said. "I'll make a cup of tea."

She seemed to have relaxed and busied herself making the tea by dropping teabags into mugs after filling the kettle. She tightened the belt of her dressing gown and turned to me after flicking the kettle's switch.

"This visitor ... what has she got to do with me?"

"He," I corrected.

She raised a brow. "He?"

I nodded. "Yes, he was looking for you. I didn't tell him anything, obviously, but I thought you'd want to know."

"Who was looking for me?"

I searched for suitable words. "Mandy ... he's one of your ... clients ..."

"Clients? I don't have any clients. What are you talking about?"

"He'd seen you on a website," I explained. "He said it was called Only Furries."

Colour rose in her cheeks, becoming a livid puce.

"He tracked you down to Haligern because of one of our bags. It was behind you in the video. He showed me ..."

She put up a hand to stop me speaking then turned to pour the boiled water into the mugs. After adding milk and taking out the teabags, she placed my mug on the table.

"I'm sorry if I've embarrassed you," I said, "but I thought you should know. You may want to call the police."

She shook her head.

"Also ... did Priscilla have an Only Furries page?"

Mandy's lips thinned. "Don't mention that bitch's name in this house."

Taken aback by the venom in her tone, and that she was speaking ill of the dead, a generally held taboo, I took a sip of tea. "I thought you were friends. You were so close at school," I said whilst watching her reaction. Something between Priscilla and Mandy had changed in the past few weeks and I wanted to get to the bottom of it. Mandy seemed to have morphed from lackey to enemy.

"That woman was rotten to the core!" she spat. "And jealous! So jealous of me that she was going to ruin everything."

"Oh?" I asked and took another sip of tea. "Would you like to tell me about it?"

Mandy's eyes narrowed. "Tell the witch about the bitch? Alright, I will. Priscilla was going to tell my husband about my page. She was so jealous that for once it was me who was more popular than her. She couldn't stand it."

"And you *were* popular. The guy who came into the shop thought you were amazing," I said. "I bet Priscilla hated that you had more fans than she did."

"She did!" Mandy's eyes glittered. "Oh, she hated it so much."

I noticed the red mark on Mandy's forearm. "That looks sore," I said. "Is it a burn?"

She pulled down the sleeve of her dressing gown to cover the red welt and gave me a furtive glance. "It's nothing, I was burning leaves in the garden yesterday."

Yesterday had been foggy with a fine drizzle, not leaf burning weather. "Priscilla's death must have been a terrible shock," I said.

Her lips pursed. "Dreadful," she said in an unconvincing tone. Her eyes caught mine before flitting to the far side of the room. "If you'll excuse me for a moment, I was about to run a bath when you knocked. I'll just check that the water's not running."

She left the room and I began to sift through the evidence. Despite Priscilla's horrible murder, Mandy had shown no sign of grief or horror over her death. She had motive. *And* she had a burn on her arm. I had all the evidence I needed. Mandy was guilty of Priscilla's murder. It struck me then that I was sitting in the kitchen of a woman who had murdered her oldest friend in cold blood and had shown not one iota of remorse. As I stood to leave, Mandy returned to the kitchen but before I had a chance to turn and face her, I was overcome by pain at the back of my head. Stumbling with the force of the blow, I staggered against the kitchen table, knocking the mug of tea to the floor before the light disappeared and blackness enveloped me.

Chapter Thirty-One

I woke to darkness and a dull but overwhelming pain in my head. Disorientated and unable to see, my breath rasped as I sucked at the air, and it took me several minutes of falling in and out of consciousness to realise that I was bound and gagged with a cover over my head. Around me I could hear voices though they made no sense. They sounded fuzzy but booming, their words slurred and incomprehensible. Nausea whorled in my belly.

I tried to move but my arms and legs were too heavy and without sensation as though I were paralysed. An effort to call out resulted in nothing. As time passed, I realised that I *was* paralysed.

I had been drugged!

Panic washed over me as realisation hit; I couldn't move or speak and only my eyes opened and closed. As my head throbbed, a chink of light caught my attention. There were gaps in the cover over my head and through them I could see movement. People were walking about illuminated in the dark by a bright light. Focusing on their voices, I began to listen to their conversations.

"What time do they light the fire, mummy?"

"In a few minutes."

"That witch is so ugly! I can't wait for her to burn."

"Can I have a hot dog mum, please!"

My heart beat with a hard and rapid pounding. I was tied to the post in the middle of the village, and it was the Night of Good Fires, the commemoration of the execution of Hetty Yikkar for witchcraft. The villagers had burned the woman at the stake—alive!

Old Mawde's grating voice repeated in my mind: 'They foretell that you will burn at the stake too! Burned to a crisp!'

I renewed my struggle and made desperate efforts to call out. "I'm here! Help! I'm here!" The words formed in my head, but my vocal chords would not cooperate. I pulled at the ropes tying my arms to the stake but only my fingers twitched.

My fingers twitched!

I focused on my feet. Would my toes move too?

No.

Focusing all effort on my fingers I felt a fizz at the fingertips. It gave me hope and the next minutes were spent in desperate efforts to get people's attention, but I only succeeded in draining my energy.

I sagged within myself and turned my attention back to the villager's conversation.

"Who's lighting the fire this year?" a woman asked. I recognised her as Kelly, the owner of the village Bed & Breakfast.

"They chose Mandy Braithwaite. Priscilla Dedman was supposed to be lighting the fire, but since she's dead, they asked her best friend to do it instead."

"Aw! That's nice," Kelly replied.

"It is, isn't it. Good turnout," her companion replied. "Bet it's good for business."

"Yes, it is! The B&B is full," Kelly replied with a happy lilt.

The noise among the crowd grew and became excited.

"They're here!" a young boy shouted.

I had never attended the Night with my aunts but had once gone with a friend and knew that a procession of villagers carrying pitchforks and other weapons walked through the streets. Several carried burning torches and the one at the front, chosen after great ceremony, would be the one to light the fire.

This year Mandy Braithwaite would be burning the witch, the second live witch burning in the village's history.

'They foretell that you will burn at the stake too!' Old Mawde cackled in my memory. 'Burned to a crisp!'

"Help!"

No sound came from my mouth.

I twitched my fingers. They gave a tiny spark that quickly fizzled.

"Help!"

A hush descended to murmurs and the hazy view I had through the fabric brightened with a yellow glow. Fire!

I sobbed and sagged against the ropes.

"It moved!" a young boy said. "Mum! Mum! The witch moved."

"It's just not tied very well, that's all," the mother replied. "It's not a real witch. Now watch! Shh!"

The villagers grew silent as the burning torch was held aloft.

"Hetty Yikkar," a man's voice boomed. "You have been found guilty of witchcraft!" The crowd jeered then grew silent. "Your punishment, to save your very soul, is to be burned to death at the stake. By the authority vested in me by the village elders, I sentence you to death." The crowd erupted with cheers and clapping. "Executioner!" he boomed. "Light the fire."

The burning light swayed and grew dim, and I heard the first crackling of twigs as they were set alight.

This was it! No one who could save me knew I was in peril. Hrok was oblivious. My Aunts had deserted me. And Garrett was away on a course.

Garrett! All of my hopes and dreams were bound to Garrett and now they would never be. I mourned for the loss of our love and sent a heartrending and silent plea to the aether.

"Garrett!" I called. "Garrett!" My voice was barely above a whisper.

The stench of burning wood seeped upwards and I felt the first heat of the fire around my feet.

I was going to burn to death, just as Priscilla had done, just as was foretold, and no one would realise until it was too late.

A scream from a villager broke through my horrified self-pity and then the crowd erupted in noise.

Fire, hot and searing, caught at my legs and I screamed in silence.

Growling mingled with the villager's shrieks.

In the next second the cover was ripped from my head, and I stared into a pair of huge amber eyes as a creature, dark and hulking, faced me. Its energy was tremendous. Standing on two legs and over six feet tall, it was muscular with broad shoulders. Its face and body were covered with dark hair and its huge hands ended in long talons.

As flames licked at my legs, it leant forwards and I felt its breath on my cheek. Muscular arms wrapped around me and I was lifted, along with the stake, out of the fire.

The beast released me from the ropes and then cradled me to its chest. I clung there, enveloped by its arms. A deafening roar was followed by shrieks as it rose to stand. Villagers scattered as the beast began to run, hugging me tight. We left the village centre, ran past the apothecary, and then headed to the fields.

For the remainder of the journey, I slipped in and out of consciousness, aware only of the night, the trees, the beast, and the searing pain in my leg. It ran through the woods, holding me to its chest as though I were nothing heavier than a small child.

When metal clanked, I opened my eyes to Blackwood manor, its gothic façade illuminated by the bright and silvery light of the full moon.

In a moment of déjà vu, the beast climbed the steps to the mansion with me cradled in its arms and hammered on the door. It grew impatient and growled then kicked the door. Seconds later the door swung open. Dizziness grew to overwhelming as the beast stepped inside the house and laid me on the sofa in Uncle Tobias' study. Amber eyes stared into mine and a huge hand cupped my face. The beast was huge, with muscular pectorals and well-defined abdominal muscles beneath a thick layer of soft hair that covered its torso and shoulders. Its head, like its body, was covered in hair and sharp canines protruded onto its lower lip. Its nose was more human than wolf-like, and its amber eyes were edged by long, dark, and curling lashes.

"Garrett," I whispered as our eyes locked.

Uncle Tobias appeared at the beast's shoulder. His face was filled with horrified pity. "I'll take care of her now, boy," he said with a tremor in his voice.

The beast growled and then I passed out.

Epilogue

Despite my insistence that my aunts not be notified of the dreadful events that had unfolded on the Night of Good Fires, word reached Aunts Thomasin, Beatrice, and Euphemia within days. They flew back to Haligern immediately and turned up on the doorstep of Blackwood Manor, brooms in hand, three nights later. Laden with creams and calmatives, they examined my wounded leg, pronounced Uncle Tobias' efforts at looking after me and my injury 'excellent' then set about making me comfortable and pandering to my every whim. Nothing was too much trouble and I picked up on more than a hint of guilt.

The full moon had passed, and Garrett was once again by my side. I had suspected he carried the Blackwood curse, but now I was certain. The truth was terrifying but I loved him just as much as before. Knowing that he was the huge and muscular creature who had saved my life gave our love an extra frisson of excitement and when I looked at him, I remembered the creature with wonderment and awe. The beast was incredible and so was Garrett. What was more wonderful was that he wanted me to be his wife.

The fire had caught my left leg from my ankle to my knee although the burn was superficial and hadn't caused serious damage. It was however painful, and in the first days as I recuperated, Garrett would carry me from room to room. In those moments I would remember the beast and how it had hugged me to its chest as we escaped the village. The beat of Garrett's heart against my cheek as he held me close gave me a thrill of joy each time.

On the fifth morning after the incident, Aunt Beatrice had applied another film of a 'curing' lotion to my leg and pronounced it much better.

"You'll be wanting to return home, Livitha," she said with a quick sideways glance at me.

My heart sank; returning home would mean leaving Garrett.

She patted my shoulder. "There will be time enough to be with him every minute of the day if you should so please, child, after you are married, but word has reached us that Editha Blackwood is on her way and it would be improper for her to find you here ... before the wedding."

"She wouldn't approve?" I asked.

Aunt Beatrice shook her head. "She would not."

"So old-fashioned!" I said with a huff of dissatisfaction.

"It is our way, and she is a stickler for tradition and protocol. The curse cast against the Blackwoods brought shame upon the family and she turned her back on magick but now ... the word is that she is working towards becoming a member of the Council. Any hint of disgrace could ruin her plans and she will not look lightly upon any faux pas on our part."

"Garrett has seemed a little nervous since a conversation he had with Uncle Tobias," I said, remembering the edge of irritability that had shown itself yesterday. "I can pack my bags and return with you," I suggested.

"It's for the best. We don't want to give her any excuse to reject the Petition."

I agreed. I couldn't bear the thought of not being able to marry Garrett. If Editha didn't give her permission and we went ahead, we would be exiled from the community, or at the very least Garrett would be barred from his inheritance. It was a future I couldn't countenance, and I had decided to be the best version of myself and give Editha Blackwood, Garrett's mother and matriarch of the family, not one reason to reject me.

Aunt Beatrice helped me to stand, and we made our way to the entrance hall where two curving staircases led to the upper floors. I had been given a suite of rooms on the same floor as Fin and Jofrid. Garrett and I hadn't been able to spend as much time with the couple as we had wanted to in the last weeks and being able to help entertain baby Soren had been a joy. The thought of leaving him was felt as a pain too.

"You'll be back soon, dear," Aunt Beatrice said, once again reading my thoughts. "And it won't be long before it's permanent." She sighed. "We will be gaining a son but losing a daughter."

Immediately torn, I placed my arm around her waist. Marrying Garrett would mean leaving my aunts.

"You can visit every day," she soothed.

As we left the sitting room and stepped into the entrance hall, a hard rapping came at the door. Uncle Tobias' butler appeared as though from thin air and the door was opened. Aunts Thomasin and Euphemia stood on the steps. Behind them I caught sight of a large black car pulling up beside Garrett's.

"Oh, Livitha!" Aunt Thomasin said as Patrick stepped aside to let her in. "Terrible news!" She waved a fold of paper in her hands.

Aunt Euphemia's face was drained of colour apart from two bright spots of pink on her cheeks made more livid by the general pallor of her skin.

"Whatever it is can wait," said Aunt Beatrice. "We need to take Livitha home. We were just on our way to pack her bags."

"But this is urgent!" said Aunt Thomasin.

At the car beside Garrett's a chauffeur in livery was holding open a door.

"What is it?" I asked as I watched a woman step out.

"Lucifer!"

The mention of my missing familiar broke the spell and I gave Aunt Thomasin my full attention. "He's not with you?"

"Whyever would he be with us?" Aunt Thomasin asked as the woman walked across the gravelled drive with the chauffeur at her side. He carried a small suitcase. Dread began to brew in my belly as I realised who the woman was.

"Well ... he wasn't at the cottage. I thought it most likely-"

"He has been kidnapped!" blurted Aunt Euphemia.

"Kidnapped?" The woman had reached the top of the steps and now stood in the open doorway.

Patrick who had been listening to our conversation turned to the door with obsequious speed. "Lady Blackwood, welcome home," he said with a slight bow.

Lady Editha Blackwood stepped over the threshold and cast her gaze among us. She settled on me with a slight frown until movement beyond my shoulder caught her attention.

"Tobias!" she said. "We appear to have a contingent of Haligern crones in the hallway!" She returned her attention to us and, with an unwelcoming frown, said. "And they appear to be causing chaos—as usual."

My heart sank as Patrick closed the door and Uncle Tobias let out a martyred sigh.

THE END

Join JC's Coven!

Join JC's Coven and get:

- **exclusive novels**
- **early access**
- **publication day notifications**
- **launch day discounts**

straight to your inbox.

Join the coven and start reading the exclusive novel, *The Lost Grimoires of Hetty Yikkar*, today!

SIGN ME UP!

https://jcblake.substack.com/

Only read paperbacks? Sign up anyway to get notifications on publication days!

Other Books by the Author

The Lost Grimoires of Hetty Yikkar[1]
Only available at JC Blake's Coven[2]
Join today. It's free!

Fascinating fantasy romance woven with magick and myth in this series of standalone novels:
Last Chance for Magic
Expecting Magic
Foretold Magic

Meet Liv and her fascinating aunts in this addictive cozy fantasy and mystery series:
Menopause, Magick, & Mystery
Hormones, Hexes, & Exes
Hot Flashes, Sorcery, & Soulmates
Night Sweats, Necromancy, & Love Bites
Menopause, Moon Magic, & Cursed Kisses
Midnight Hexes & Gathering Storms

---

1. *https://jcblake.substack.com/s/the-lost-grimoires-of-hetty-yikkar*

2. https://jcblake.substack.com/

Midnight Hexes & Hormonal Exes
Midlife Curses & Lovestruck Shifters
Harems, Hexes, & Hairy Housewives
Merry Widows & Cantankerous Crones
Midlife Nuptials & Hexed Honeymoons

Meet Leofe, the Poison Garden Witch, as she discovers her
magical powers and makes life after divorce an adventure:
Poison Garden Witch series
Deadheading the Hemlock
Pruning the Wolfsbane

A young woman is pushed to the edge of a breakdown in this
supernatural murder mystery:
When the Dead Weep

Printed in Great Britain
by Amazon

21219764R00150